SCIENCE FICTION STORIES AND MORE   OCTOBER 2023

DARKMATTER

MAGAZINE

First paperback edition October 2023.

Edited by Rob Carroll
Cover art by Devin Forst
Cover design by Rob Carroll
Layout by Rob Carroll

Interior art by Miranda Mundt copyright © 2023,
Dennis Preston copyright © 2023,
Adobe Stock copyright © 2023
Photos courtesy of Hoss Fatemi, Phil McLaughlin, Dennis Preston
Promotional images courtesy of Phil McLaughlin, Harper Collins, and William Morrow
Printed by permission.

Printed by Ingram Content Group

ISBN 979-8-8689-6184-7 (paperback)

Dark Matter Magazine
P.O. Box 372
Wheaton, IL 60187

darkmattermagazine.com
darkmattermagazine.shop

SCIENCE FICTION STORIES AND MORE   OCTOBER 2023

DARKMATTER
MAGAZINE

DARK
MATTER

darkmattermagazine.com
darkmattermagazine.shop

MAMA

by Devin Forst

"Children should never have baths," my grandmother said. "It's a dangerous habit."
"I agree, Grandmamma."

—Roald Dahl
The Witches

Pictured left: *Mama*

DARK MATTER STAFF

Rob Carroll
Editor-in-Chief

Anna Madden
Acquisitions Editor

Marie Croke
Acquisitions Editor

Marissa van Uden
Acquisitions Editor

Maddy Leary
Production Editor

Phil McLaughlin Director of Media	**Jena Brown** Features Writer
Alli Nesbit Audio Director	**Janelle Janson** Features Writer
Olly Jeavons Illustrator	**Eric Carroll** Media Relations

CONTENTS

LETTER FROM THE EDITOR

MONTER MASH   11
Rob Carroll

FICTION

CAT'S EYE   15
Aia Järvinen

THE GIFT HORSE'S MOUTH   31
Zachary Olson

STATION 99   37
Amanda Cecelia Lang

GOD'S WATCHFUL EYES   61
Grace R. Reynolds

GHOUL   67
Victoria Nations

LIZARD MAN   77
Polly Hall

DEVIL CHILD   85
Kay Hanifen

HOTEL LEVIATHAN: THE DICHOTOMY OF A BEAST   105
Eygló Karlsdóttir

RETSNOM 113
Rowan Hill

TO DIE A MONSTER 121
Samuel Poots

REPRINT FICTION

ONE LAST STEP 139
Warren Benedetto

AUTHOR INTERVIEWS

PAUL TREMBLAY 131
Feature by Janelle Janson

ART FEATURES

COVER ART 5
Devin Forst

(UN)MUTED 53
Miranda Mundt

TOAD BOYS 95
Dennis Preston

MONSTER MASH

by Rob Carroll

"I've just always liked monsters, since I was a little kid. It was always the thing I found interesting. It's always what I wanted to draw; it's always what I wanted to read, and so, yeah, I don't know. It's a good question for a therapist, why I like monsters. But I tend not to question it. It's what pays the bills, so that's kind of nice."

—*Mike Mignola*
Creator of Hellboy

"Monster" has many different connotations. For example, a serial killer is a monster, but so is a six-foot-four, 250-pound, All-Pro linebacker with the power to terrorize NFL quarterbacks. Jason Voorhees is a monster, but so is Mike Wazowski from *Monsters, Inc.* Something can be monstrous in appearance, like the Chimera of Greek myth, or exclusively monstrous in action, like Patrick Bateman from *American Psycho.* Some might even label you a monster for littering that one time in a public park.

But for the sake of this essay, let's set aside the connotative dependence and turn instead to the musings of eighteenth-century romantic painter, Francisco Goya, who once claimed that it is Reason in creation that separates monsters from marvels. According to Goya, imagination united with reason creates marvels, while imagination abandoned by reason creates monsters.

I think Goya is right, and I believe it's this close relationship between romance and tragedy, order and chaos, good and evil, the possible and impossible, that makes monsters so interesting, even relatable. Every one of us struggles with physical and emotional flaws, with the unenviable choices we've made, with sin; and every one of us has abandoned reason at some point in our lives. Sure, most of us want to be heroes, but in many stories, we're unwittingly cast as the villain. Sometimes, we even cast ourselves in that role, and sometimes, we even like it.

We need to confront our own bad behavior, both in the kinetic state and the potential, and monsters help us do this in three ways: 1) They help us identify humanity's darker impulses, to acknowledge them by name, and hopefully, to help us cast them back into the pit, triumphant; 2) They help us challenge our preconceived notions about the world and teach us that perception is not always reality, that what seems unreasonable is not (the warbling bray of a murderous space-Bigfoot doesn't have to be terrifying—just ask Han Solo); and 3) The worst monsters, the most viscerally terrifying, the ones that hate simply to hate, remind us that true evil *does* exist and that it cannot be understood, only rebuked—the abandonment of reason, as Goya would say, is the point.

But setting aside the truly vile creatures that haunt this world, most monsters are just a whole lot of fun. They're explorations of the odd, the strange, the comically exaggerated. They spook us, creep us out, cause us to shudder, shiver, and jump. They make us tilt our heads and cast a gimlet eye upon the page or screen. Some are funny, some are even cute. Some cause us to question everything we know about biology, psychology, and basic Euclidean geometry. But most of all, they're imagination united with reason—with purpose—and this makes them marvels.

In this, the third annual Halloween Special Issue of *Dark Matter Magazine*, eleven stories spin thrilling tales of monsters good, bad, and complicated. In "Cat's Eye" by Aia Järvinen, a monster in life is a monster in death, but lucky for us, the veil between worlds is thin and many creatures of this realm can see right through it. In "The Gift Horse's Mouth" by Zachary Olson, the most terrifying kind of monster is the one that lives quietly among us, the one who looks you in the eye and smiles before they plunge the knife. In "Station 99" by Amanda Cecelia Lang, the reasoned monsters of our collective imaginations are made irrational and turned against us, but if something is beyond reason, is it also beyond defeat? In "God's Watchful Eyes" by Grace R. Reynolds, a fallen world is no refuge for the wicked. Monsters want a world filled with prey, not competing predators. In "Ghoul" by Victoria

Nations, "Lizard Man" by Polly Hall, and "Demon Child" by Kay Hanifen, we're reminded how useless it is to judge a person's character based solely on the assumptions built into society's archetypal memory; a kind heart has no single defining form, nor does a monstrous one. In "Hotel Leviathan," author Eygló Karlsdóttir illustrates the slow-moving momentum of evil and the way it gains power not through subjugation but through willing participation, and how disillusionment comes too late. In "retsnoM" by Rowan Hill, an arrogant man who manipulates the people around him must now defeat a cosmic monster that has the power to make him its literal puppet. What a handsome trophy such a silver-tongued thing would make, they both think. In "To Die a Monster" by Samuel Poots, another puppet laments his role in the deaths of so many innocents, but a man without free will cannot be a sinner, only a tool of some other being's sin, as is shown when he starts to reclaim his autonomy and assert his true nature. And finally, in this issue's reprint story "One Last Step" by Warren Benedetto, a little girl learns that prey can only hide for so long before they get slaughtered. To defeat monsters, she must become one—an apex predator on the hunt.

Sincerely,
Rob Carroll
Editor-in-Chief

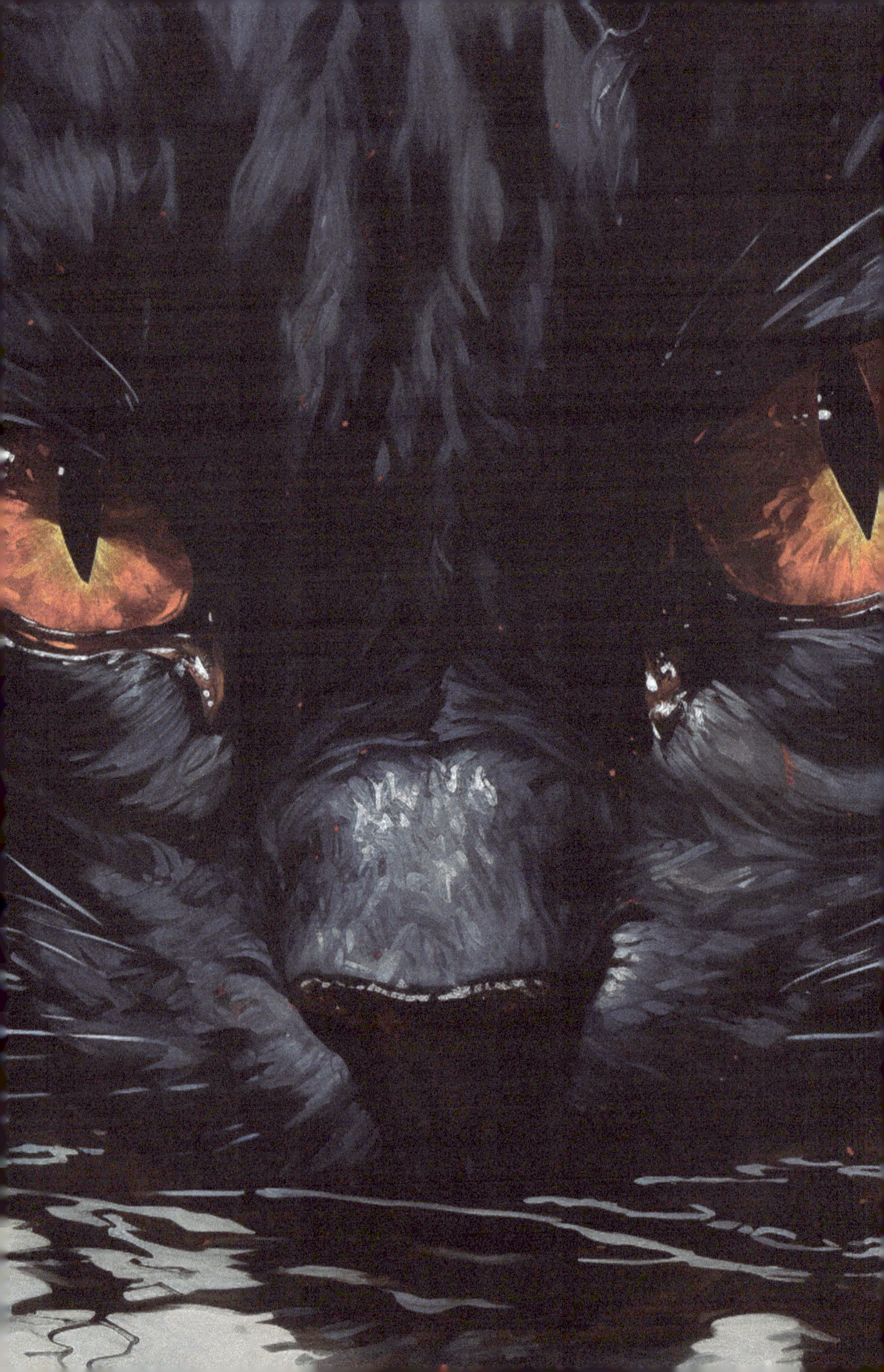

CAT'S EYE

by Aia Järvinen

Damien was the most gorgeous cat Samantha had ever seen. His silken, atramentous coat caught the faintest light, and those mesmerizing green eyes shone more brightly than the quartz stones resembling them. The seven-pound Bombay was too regal for a stray who'd wandered out of nowhere and chosen her as his human. She often wondered where he'd come from, but cats never shared their secrets.

"What do you think, buddy? Does our new apartment pass inspection?" she asked, watching the cat padding around the room.

Damien didn't acknowledge her questions. He was engrossed in the second phase of his post-move reconnaissance, sniffing everything he'd already sniffed the previous night. Stalking the room's perimeter, he made no sound but for the occasional low growl when he smelled something strange.

Probably a previous tenant's pet, Samantha thought.

"It's an old house, buddy," she said, in a tone she hoped would ease his palpable tension. "A lot of people have lived here since the Victorian era. It must be sensory overload for your little sniffer, huh?"

He looked to her, and she saw the staggering intelligence behind those green eyes. She could've sworn he understood every word she said.

Grace, beauty, intelligence—it was no wonder why feline deification spanned centuries, continents, and cultures. China had its *shíshī* guardian lions. Japanese folklore was filled with mischievous *kaibyō*. Cats held every mythical rank from pulling Freya's chariot to embodying anthropomorphic Egyptian gods. Barbara—Samantha's Muslim friend from high school— had once told her that angels wouldn't enter a home with a dog, but that cats were revered in Islam for their cleanliness.

Samantha smiled at Damien. "You're not some deity or guardian spirit or anything like that, are you?"

He gave her a look that said all cats considered themselves gods.

"Of course," she scoffed at herself. "Dumb question."

Damien growled again, flicking his tail and twitching his nose at a few white paint chips that'd bubbled and peeled off the windowsill. He shot across the floor to scrutinize a matte patch of raw wood where the varnish had cracked and broken away. A few of the narrow planks bowed upwards, evidence of water damage from an indecipherable time ago.

"I know. It's not exactly what I was hoping for, but the price is right."

The two-story house had been converted into four apartments. Theirs was the lower left quadrant, when facing the house from the street. It was just enough space for a twenty-three-year-old and her furry companion and was within walking distance of the restaurant where she worked. The other three tenants were older male business types who were unlikely to disturb her reading on days off. She could deal with the earthy smell and groans of expanding wood if it meant avoiding the loud, drunken partying common to other apartments in the city.

Inspection complete, Damien trotted back across the room and leapt onto Samantha's lap. He revved his engine to report that the residence was secure. For such a small guy, he had a powerful motor.

"Jeez, you didn't come with a muffler, did you?" Samantha stroked his sleek back.

Damien arched his spine beneath her black nails and turned in a circle on her lap before sitting facing her.

"Typical," she said, shaking her head at him. "You only want to cuddle when I need to leave for work."

Her gaze drifted across the modest living space to the unpacked boxes filled with their sparse belongings—her books, his toys. Most of her closet was strewn over the few pieces of furniture she owned.

"I'll try to finish unpacking tonight, but I need to go. That jerk put me on another double shift. Take care of the house today while I'm gone.

Okay, buddy?" Samantha scratched his fluffy neck with both hands and smooshed his face.

Damien's purr kicked into overdrive. It wasn't his usual breathy purr-rest, purr-rest. The trill was deep and steady, threatening. It sounded more like his growl.

Samantha's hands froze but remained loosely cupping the cat's face as his slim tail bristled. A ridge of raised hair fanned down his spine. His pupils dilated—vitreous black swallowing the bright green—but his eyes weren't on her.

They glared over her shoulder.

She squinted, thinking she saw movement in those black mirrors, but she couldn't decipher it. The tall shadow seemed to be moving—no, *writhing*, while simultaneously standing still. A rank stench hit her olfactory receptors and Samantha covered her nose and mouth before she retched.

Damien released a protracted hiss, baring his maw of enamel-coated needles.

Samantha whipped her head to the right, still covering her nose as she looked over her shoulder. Her heartbeat hammered against her ribs, her pits damp. The fine hairs on her arms stood erect. Her dark eyes searched for any possible source of the unnerving reflection.

All she saw was the blank wall.

"What the hell was that?" She looked back to the cat. "You scared me."

Damien gave a short, indignant trill, offended that she dared question his instinct. His pupils had contracted to their customary slits, fangs sheathed within his fuzzy jowls.

"I guess moving has us both on edge. It was probably just a shadow from a passing car. The smell must've come from the house's crawl space. All those bare patches let the smell come right up. There's gotta be all kinds of vermin living under there. Good thing I have a vicious guard cat to protect me."

Samantha gave Damien's head several quick smooches before standing and setting him on the blanket that covered the couch. She grabbed her bag and strode for the door, saying, "I'll see you tonight, buddy. Be a good boy."

Damien watched her leave with an imperial expression that said he was always a good boy.

Locking the apartment door behind her, Samantha pushed open the house's main door and hurried down the stone steps to the sun-drenched sidewalk. The May morning greeted her with a heavy dose of humid heat that produced instant sweat on the back of her neck and made her dyed-black curls stick to her skin. The restaurant's kitchen would be near unbearable.

Three boys were passing on their way to school. She guessed they were probably ten or eleven. The boy in the lead stopped, and his two companions followed suit.

"You live here?" the lead boy asked, eyeing her and then the house.

He wore a black T-shirt with a clown on it—Captain Something—from a horror movie the title of which escaped her. The boy's greasy, light brown hair made weak waves around his pale face.

"Yes, why?" she asked.

"Don't you know this place is haunted?" Clown Shirt asked.

She resisted the urge to roll her eyes. "Most of the buildings in this town have a reputation for being haunted. It's a ploy to get more tourism."

"No, this place is *really* haunted. Haven't you heard of the Worm Man?"

"Like the Mothman? You could've come up with something more original if you wanted to scare me."

"I didn't come up with it. My granddad told me about it. He said the original owners were a married couple who rented out rooms, but that the husband couldn't keep away from the single babes who stayed here. He'd use his master key and sneak into their rooms at night to *have his way with them*." Clown Shirt wiggled his eyebrows for effect.

"Do you even know what that phrase means?" Samantha asked. She sure as hell wasn't going to explain it to him.

"It's true, though," said one of the other boys. His curly black hair was cut short. His smooth, walnut skin was yet to show signs of puberty acne. "The guy got away with it for decades."

Samantha couldn't imagine why Clown Shirt's grandfather had told him such a story or why she bothered listening.

"When the wife found out, she went postal," the third boy added. His fine red hair and freckles, combined with his Slipknot T-shirt, made him look like a heavy metal Opie Taylor.

"She pushed him down the stairs to break his legs, then stabbed him a bajillion times with a kitchen knife," said Metal Opie. The other two boys made *Psycho* sound effects and stabbing gestures to illustrate. "The old bat buried his half-dead ass under the house and let the creepy-crawlies slowly eat him to death."

"Good for her," Samantha replied, unfazed.

"Except he didn't die," Clown Shirt said, taking over narration again. "They say he's so evil, he sucks life from all the animals living under there—that worms ate his skin and now squirm all over his rotting muscles to help him stand."

A twinge of unease seized her stomach. Had she heard this story somewhere? It was starting to feel familiar, but she couldn't place it in her memory. Looking back to the house, she saw Damien watching her from the front window.

"I heard giant worms fused with what's left of his face and hang off his skull like that octopus-headed captain in the second *Pirates* movie," Curly said.

"He's still alive down there," Metal Opie added, without missing a beat, "waiting to satisfy his eternal need, waiting for a hot babe like *you.*"

The compatriots made spooky sound effects in stereo, followed by uncontainable laughter.

Samantha almost applauded their performance. For a second, they'd nearly had her. She didn't have the heart to point out the major flaws in the Worm Man's story, such as: 1) the unlikelihood that anything would be left of a hundred and something-year-old corpse except bones; 2) that worms were not strong nor intelligent enough to work in synchronization; and 3) that Clown Shirt's granddad was full of horse excrement.

"Well, it's too bad for the Worm Man, then," Samantha said, "because I'm into girls."

The boys stared at her with slack jaws. Before she could say anything more, her phone vibrated. She looked at the lock screen and saw a text from her boss, then saw the time.

"Damn it!"

Samantha sprinted down the street. The Worm Man story fled her mind as she focused on the opening duties she'd have to perform in turbo mode if she wanted to save her hide. She didn't hear when Clown Shirt yelled after her.

"Don't let the Worm Man get you!"

Stomping up the shadowy front steps, Samantha let herself into the house and resisted slamming the door behind her. The restaurant's kitchen closed at 9 p.m., but the dishwasher had bailed at eight without telling anyone, and the two line cooks went out to smoke and never came back, leaving Samantha to close alone. The situation was getting too common for her liking—a little hazing from her male colleagues who wanted to ensure she knew there'd be no special treatment simply because she had two *x* chromosomes. She couldn't tell the boss, or they'd accuse her of being too moody, hormonal, or some other offensive stereotype to misdirect blame. They'd done it before.

Damien meowed in greeting as she entered. He performed his customary prancing dance with his tail at attention while twisting his head back and forth, keeping his green eyes on her.

"Hey, buddy. I'm glad to see you too." She kicked off her work shoes, lest she track fryer grease through the apartment.

The cat galloped across the room and disappeared behind a few boxes, returning with some kind of striped ribbon in his mouth.

"Aww, did you find a toy?" Samantha crooned, crouching to extend her hand. "Bring it to me and I'll play with you before I shower."

Damien ran to her and deposited the trophy on her palm.

Samantha gasped. She dropped the slithering ribbon and shot to standing, shuffling backwards until she hit the wall.

The cat pounced on the snake, pinning it with both paws. Damien bit the serpent's middle and threw his head side-to-side, making it flail.

"Take it outside!" Samantha shrieked. She ran down the narrow hallway and yanked open the back door. "Damien! Outside!"

The cat dashed down the hallway—his eyes shining with predatory glee— and shot out the doorway. He launched off the top step of the weathered deck and landed on the concrete driveway, triggering the motion sensor light. Samantha looked away, not wanting to witness what happened next and not caring, provided that the cat left the carcass outside.

Taking a step towards her bedroom, her right foot squished something slippery and slid a few inches before she threw her arms out to grasp the doorframe for support. Samantha bent her knee, twisting her leg so she could look at the bottom of her sock. She instantly wished she hadn't. Seeping through the dirty cotton to violate the sole of her foot was the glistening slime that'd once been a plump snail.

Samantha released a wordless vocalization of revulsion, contorting in a full-body cringe as she clenched her eyes shut and used a single fingertip to peel off the sock before tossing it into the night.

"Gross, gross, gross, gross, gross!" she moaned, then froze.

Wait a second. Snakes, snails…

She gasped in indignation. "Oh, those little *devils*."

The boys. They must've broken into her apartment after school and left their gifts for her to find. It wouldn't have been hard. Half the aged windows didn't lock—the latches having rusted and broken—and the back door was nothing but a knob with a lock. No deadbolt. An easy thing to pick. Back in college, she would use her library card to pick a similar lock to her dorm room. Modern boys were undoubtedly more sophisticated in their methods.

Your little trick didn't work, gentlemen, she thought, narrowing her eyes at their memory. *I'm not falling for it. Worm Man, indeed!*

Damien strutted back inside, looked up at her, and licked his jowls.

Samantha stood at the front window the following morning, stroking Damien in her arms with the focus of a woman on a mission. She watched all the neighborhood kids make their book-laden treks to the school down the street. When she saw a familiar trio approaching, she kissed the cat's head and left him inside while she exited to greet them.

Clown Shirt saw her first and exclaimed, "Look who survived the night!"

"So it *was* you," Samantha said.

"It was us, what?" Clown Shirt asked. He wore a different shirt today, one with a yellow smiley face that bled from a bullet hole between its eyes, but that didn't matter to Samantha. From now on, he would always just be Clown Shirt to her.

"You three pranked me, didn't you? You broke into my house while I was at work and left me your little *gifts.*"

"What you talkin' about, lady?" Curly asked.

"There was a snake in my apartment last night, *and* a giant snail. If I find any puppy dog tails, I'm calling PETA."

"Is she crazy?" Metal Opie asked the others, keeping his eyes on her.

"Don't play innocent with me, Lords of the Flies. I know what boys are like. You think you're funny, don't you?"

"Whatever you think we did, it wasn't us," Clown Shirt said.

"We weren't near your stupid apartment. We all got picked up right after school and went to our friend's birthday party. His mom'll tell you we were there. Call her," Metal Opie said.

Samantha searched their faces for lies and saw none.

Was it just a fluke? The house is *old. It wouldn't be the first apartment I've had with the occasional critter issue.*

"She strokin' out or something?" Curly asked. "Should we call 9-1-1?"

"I'm fine. Maybe I jumped to conclusions. Sorry for accusing you."

"Can we go? We're gonna be late for school." Clown Shirt said, pointing towards the long walk ahead of them.

Samantha lifted her left arm in a gesture of dismissal. As the boys passed, she heard Metal Opie whisper, "Girls are weird."

Mortified by her overreaction, Samantha spent Friday's shift on sullen autopilot. She didn't even grumble to herself when the dishwasher and two line cooks bailed on her again. She just checked off the closing sheet and ensured the restaurant's back door locked behind her.

"Hey, buddy," she said to Damien, upon entering the apartment. "Sorry I couldn't come visit you on break. The lunch rush ran right into dinner. It felt like everyone in town got off work early."

The house was silent but for Damien's urgent pleas for attention.

Good. No one will disturb me if I go to bed early. She turned for the hallway and halted, her eyes widening.

The floor was smeared with brown paste. Even the walls were stained with the stuff, like someone had dragged their messy fingers down the clean white paint. Samantha's head whipped to Damien.

"Did those boys do this? Did they lie to me?"

The cat released a loud cry as though to say it wasn't his fault.

"Sleeping on the job, huh? I thought you were some powerful guardian kitty. How could you let them prank me again?"

Damien grunted low and trotted off to his cat tree to keep sentry.

"Please only be mud, please only be mud," she chanted, forcing herself to crouch low enough to sniff the sludge.

Samantha exhaled in relief. "It's mud."

Damien licked his paw and washed his pristine face.

"It's a pity you don't have opposable thumbs. You could help me clean." She pulled the black kitchen gloves up her forearms and set to scrubbing.

Her work shirt was damp with perspiration by the time she finished, her back sore and face oily. Stretching herself to standing, she lumbered down the hallway to the bathroom and massaged oil cleanser over her skin. It was pricey—imported from Japan—but it was the only thing that'd remove her makeup. Samantha turned on the hot water tap and leaned over just in time to get an eyeful of worms writhing and wriggling in the drain.

She cried out, slapped the water tap off, and shuffled backwards until she tripped and landed on her tailbone inside the tub.

Damien charged into the room with an urgent trill that said *I'll handle this* and flew onto the countertop. He clawed at the basin, his pupils as wide as the druggies' she worked with. He growled and clawed, growled and clawed.

"Don't—" she choked, unsure of what she was telling the cat not to do. Not to save her from the Worm Man? She barked a laugh at her own ridiculousness. It was a bad prank from lying little boys, nothing more.

Samantha wriggled out of the tub and inched closer to peek into the sink. All she saw was an empty drain.

"What the…" She looked to the cat. "Did I imagine it?"

Damien made a few more padding motions on the porcelain and wiggled his little butt before charging out of the room again in full zoomy mode.

"Crackhead," she grumbled after him. "I'm cutting back your catnip allowance."

Though she knew in her bones that it was a prank, Samantha found sleep an elusive companion that night. Whenever she was on the verge of slumber, she would hear a strange noise, like the creak of shifting floorboards, a pop of ice crashing from the ice maker into the holding tray, or a moan that could've only been a gust of wind.

It's all in your head, she reminded herself, turning onto her left side in bed. Her eyes drifted open against her will and fixed on the window shade. Her breath caught in her lungs, and she dived for the bedside lamp.

The sudden light eradicated the shadow she'd seen against her bedroom window, that backlit hulking figure too large for a mere boy. Maybe all three had huddled together to savor her unease. Sheer adrenaline forced her to the window, and Samantha peeked outside, expecting to see them giggling in the bushes. The driveway's motion sensor light was still on. That light only came on when creatures Damien's size or larger passed beneath its cyclops eye.

She couldn't see a single animal outside.

Samantha growled in frustration and fell back into bed, pressing a pillow over her head. Didn't boys have anything better to do on a Friday night than torment a stranger?

Saturday passed in a blur. It was her third double shift in a row and the busiest day of the week, as the restaurant offered brunch. The town's upper crust drove down from their mansions to sip iced coffee and munch on eggs Benedict, enjoying the shade before returning across the street to the park, where the farmer's market bustled with commerce.

The brunch crowd segued to the binge-drinking crowd, and Saturday nights were always bets-off. There was no telling who'd puke mid-karaoke or get thrown out for trying to grope the waitstaff, who'd decide to break up with her boyfriend before a buzzed audience or announce to her best friend that she'd slept with her husband. Samantha preferred drama to remain between the pages of her favorite books. Sometimes, Saturdays felt like she was trapped in a bad reality TV show, though reality was growing more surreal by the day.

Samantha's legs trembled as she entered the apartment, her gaze shooting in every direction, searching for signs of break-ins or vandalism. Part of her wished the boys would leave evidence. A keychain, a pressed penny from a school field trip to the zoo, anything that proved recent events were the work of three teenage humans.

She found nothing. No critters, no mud. No shadows.

"Maybe they got bored and found someone better to torment." She hoped so.

Samantha stripped, dropping articles of clothing as she padded towards the shower. Her feet felt like chicken breasts flattened by a tenderizer. A hot shower and a good sleep, that's what she needed.

Standing beneath the flow, she let the steam and spray calm her nerves and relax her body. She forced herself to breathe deeply, knowing she'd fall fast asleep once her warmed body cooled. Inhale…exhale…inhale— Samantha gagged.

There was that rank smell again, like rotting meat. She'd smelled it once at another restaurant, where no one had abided by the FIFO method. There was no meat in her house.

Something was wrong with the water. It felt too thick as it splattered against her hair. Samantha opened her eyes and saw multiple brown streams shooting towards her face. She groaned in disgust and backed against the shower wall.

The mud dissipated, the water running clear again.

You're okay, she told herself, as mud slid down her cheekbones. *It's just the city. They must've messed with the water supply today. You've seen brown water before. Calm down. It's not life or death. It's just gross.*

Samantha scrubbed her body until she looked like a lobster. Slipping into a T-shirt and shorts, she crawled into bed but couldn't sleep. The faintest noise sent her heart rate rocketing. She clutched Damien to her chest and repeated the mantras that failed to calm her.

It's just the boys.

It's only the city.

It's all in your head.

Sunday, her precious day off, was a bust.

Whenever she tried to read, the words squirmed and slithered across the pages. The air smelled like rotten meat every time the AC kicked on. The slightest shifting of wood made her jump. Damien growling at every corner didn't help.

She'd spent the night watching the windows, determined to catch the boys in the act. All she'd succeeded in accomplishing was losing more sleep. She hadn't spied a single boy.

"Something's not right," Samantha said to Damien. "Kids get bored easily. Even if they pranked me, they'd have moved on by now."

Damien continued methodically cleaning himself, seemingly oblivious to her distress.

Unease got the better of her. Samantha grabbed her phone and called the landlady.

"Hi, Mrs. Kilkenny. This is Samantha. Apartment three? I just had a couple questions about the house. Is this a good time?"

"Sure, dear. What would you like to know?" the older woman asked through the line.

"How long have you owned this property?" she asked, tapping a black nail against her thigh.

"Why, it's been in my family for a few generations now."

"Have there ever been any…unusual occurrences?"

The woman paused a fraction of a second too long. That pause confirmed Samantha's fears. Her stomach felt like an implosion.

She knows there's something wrong with the house. She knows, and she let me sign the lease anyway.

"Unusual occurrences?" the woman asked, feigning ignorance. "Like what?"

"I…I've been having some plumbing issues." It was all she could think to say to escape the conversation. If this woman knew of her undead ancestor and his wiles, she wasn't going to admit it. It also meant she wasn't going to help.

"Oh, *that*. Well, old pipes, you know. I'll have my man stop by this week."

"Sure," Samantha whispered.

Hanging up with a shaking hand, she looked to Damien. "I can't sleep here. Should I try calling Laura and see if she'll let us stay a few nights?"

Damien gave her a disparaging look.

"You're right. I forgot she's allergic to cats. That little escapade didn't end well, either. I could try smuggling you into a hotel."

The cat placed a gentle paw on her forearm, as though reassuring her that he was there, that it'd be okay.

She smiled through her fear. "Thanks, buddy. At least I have you looking out for me."

The Monday morning sunlight felt like acid in the backs of her throbbing ocular cavities. Her unwashed hair coiled in matted tendrils around her shoulders, skin cold despite the heat. Puddles of smeared makeup accented the dark shadows beneath her eyes. Her nail polish was chipped from hours scratching at the floorboards, looking for chinks to plug. She'd left Damien inside, but beside her on the top step was the weighty meat cleaver that went everywhere with her now—at least, everywhere around the house.

She saw the boys' slack jaws from yards away, the *o*'s of their mouths growing larger as they approached and stopped before her.

"Hey, lady, you okay? You don't look too good." Curly said.

"No, I'm not okay," she said, rising on perfidious legs. "I need you to be honest with me. Was—*Is* there really a Worm Man? Did you really hear that story from your grandfather? It sounds like something you probably saw on that *Stranger Stuff* show."

"*Stranger Things*," Curly corrected her, enunciating *things*.

"Is weird stuff still happening to you?" Clown Shirt asked, his young brow creased with concern.

"Like you don't know."

"We don't. We've been camping all weekend."

No, you couldn't have been. You're the only reasonable explanation. It must be you.

"What happened now?" Clown Shirt asked.

She scrutinized their faces. Their former teasing expressions had morphed to concern. Metal Opie's wide blue eyes looked downright terrified as she described the recent disturbances.

"Holy crap! That stuff actually happened?" Clown Shirt asked.

"*Yes.*"

"Look, lady—"

"Samantha."

"We really didn't do it," Curly said. "Sounds like my granddad was right. You'd better move. You don't want some dead guy's worms."

She didn't want a live guy's worm near her, let alone the worms of some perpetually rotting urban legend with a thing for younger women. Sleep deprivation compounded her paranoia and eroded her rationality. Recent events almost had her believing in the Worm Man.

Something was messing with her.

Samantha looked to Clown Shirt. "Is there anything else you can tell me about that story?"

"I told you everything Granddad told me. Are you gonna be okay? Can you get away somewhere? You already look half dead," he said, ever the charmer.

I can't get away. I signed a contract, and I can't afford to live anywhere else. I have to stay here if it kills me.

In a rare gesture of goodwill, Samantha's boss sent her home early Monday night with the order to get some sleep. She figured he was tired of her nicking herself from working while delirious and wanted to avoid writing an accident report. Whatever the reason, she gratefully staggered through the dark streets back to the house.

She took a bath, too fatigued to care whether or not the brown stuff she bathed in was mud. She just relaxed in the hot water and let it massage her tense muscles, knotted from days of work, stress, and anxiety. Her adrenaline was tapped out. She couldn't stay awake another night. Sleep deprivation had her seeing writhing shadows everywhere.

Samantha shuffled across the narrow corridor and fell into bed without bothering to dry her hair or find clothes. She pulled the fuzzy blanket around her body, which only seemed to insulate her fears.

It's just a myth. It's not real. You're okay. You're going to be okay. You just need rest.

Damien leapt onto the bed and curled into a circle of floof atop her thighs. His deep, reassuring purrs lulled her to sleep.

Samantha dreamed of impossible extant musculature straining over sickening yellow bones to churn the soil beneath her bed, of dermis composed entirely of worms, and of heavy, fetid breaths too cold for a living mammal. She dreamed of an emaciated arm reaching towards her body in jerky movements with nothing but a few moldering planks between them.

The warped floor shifted like a puzzle box, allowing the undead creature through.

Damien's yowl wrenched her conscious and Samantha's eyes shot open. She lunged forward into a sitting position and fumbled for the bedside lamp. Light flooded the little room.

Samantha's voice fled too deep within her to scream. Her mind glitched, refusing to accept what her wide eyes beheld. All she could do was stare.

Damien looked up at her with a mouthful of worms, the foul remains of what lay slaughtered on the floor reflected in his gleaming eyes.

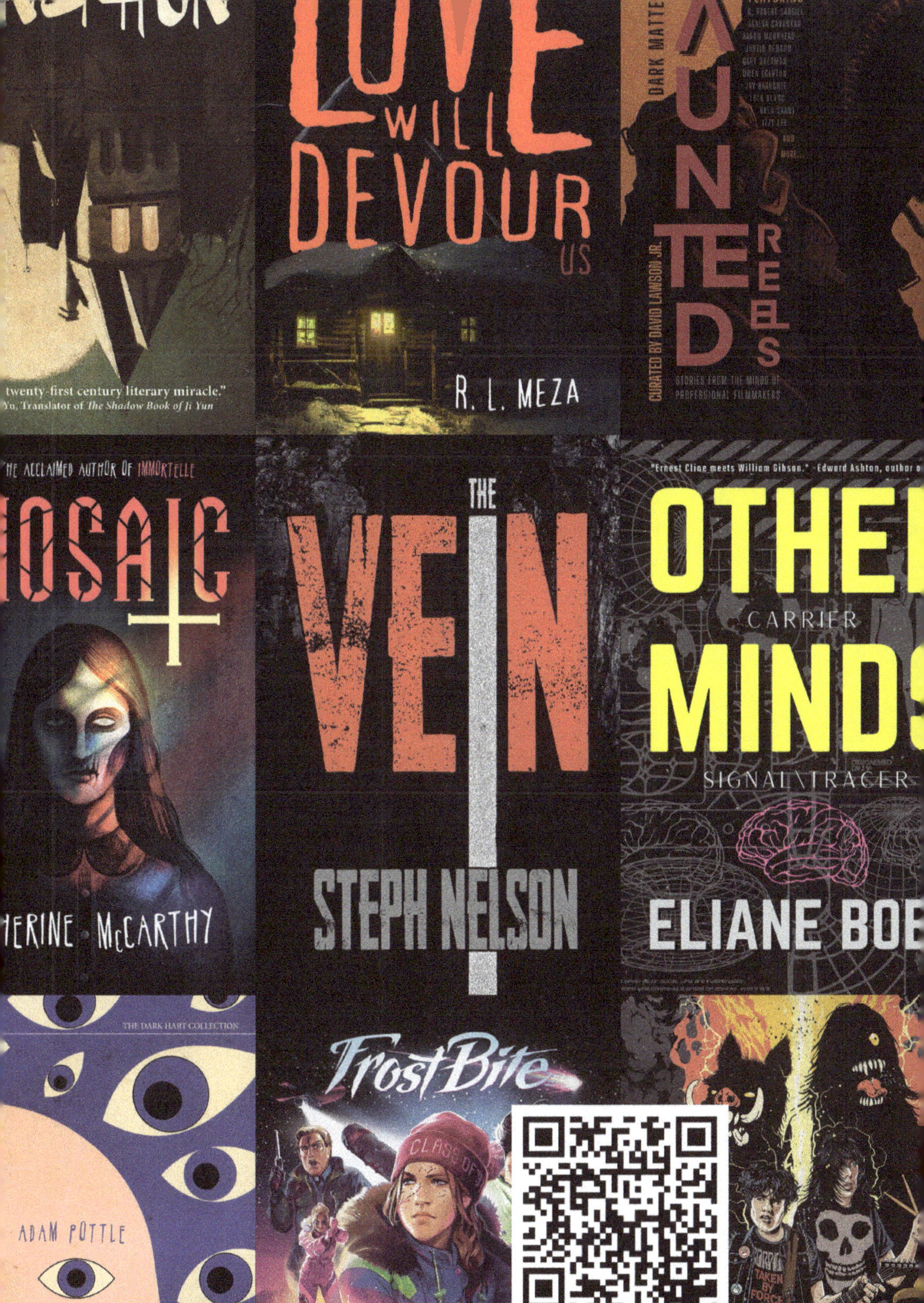

THE GIFT HORSE'S MOUTH

by Zachary Olson

When I finally finished my apprentice-ship with Enzo Benedetti, the greatest locksmith I've ever known, he sat me down on an old teak chair in his office. He gave me a cigar, a glass of port, and three pieces of advice:

1. Never open a lock shop across from another smith.

2. Always keep a record of every key you cut, every single time.

3. Never, under any circumstances, should you take a house call for a rich man.

The third one tripped me up.

"Enzo," I said. "Don't I want to do business with rich folks?"

Enzo grinned around his stogie, evening sunlight throwing chiaroscuro shadows across the canyons of his face.

"Business, sure. But going to a rich man's house? A big old mansion with a dozen rooms and God knows what else? Never in your life, kid. You know why?"

"Why?" I asked, young and stupid. Enzo took a long pull on his cigar, a modern-day Socrates blessing his Plato.

"It's simple, Rahul, my boy. Because rich folks are fucking crazy."

"I can't thank you enough for coming all the way out here, Mister Bhatt."

Denise Toussaint smiled down from the threshold. I looked up at her, only halfway up the porch when she'd opened the door. She must have been waiting; I figured she was nervous.

Missus Toussaint was a delicate-looking lady, all porcelain skin and flaxen hair in a dress so plain it *had* to be expensive. She reminded me a bit of the dress-up dolls my sister had when we were kids, back before they made dolls that looked like us, back when she had to make do with an endless parade of blondes and brunettes.

"Of course, Missus Toussaint." I smiled as gently as I could, trying to put her at ease. "You have a lovely home," I added as she ushered me inside.

The Toussaint house was a three-story colonial mansion. It sat on the very edge of the greater metropolitan area, past where the suburbs gave way to wetlands and civilization threw up its hands and turned to greener pastures. It was huge and creepy and old, but I'd just driven two hours to get there, so it was beautiful.

Denise shut the door behind me as I craned my neck to take in the foyer. It had one of those crystal chandeliers that you only see in movies. I counted half a dozen burnt-out bulbs.

"I hope you didn't have a hard time finding the place, Mister Bhatt," said Missus Toussaint, sidling up beside me.

"Well, it was either the house or the lake," I said, "So I figured my chances were solid." She laughed heartily at that, putting a hand on my arm and squeezing. Maybe she wasn't as nervous as I'd thought.

Upstairs, something thumped. I jumped, head whipping toward the noise. The second-floor landing was empty.

"Mister Bhatt?" Denise's voice was honeyed with concern. I turned back to her.

"I think your dog knocked something over up there," I said. She tilted her head.

"Dog, Mister Bhatt?" she asked. "I don't have a dog."

"Your cat, then?"

Denise looked back at me blankly, then smiled wide. "Oh, you mean the house settling? Don't worry about that, Mister Bhatt. It's an old place, after all. It's got a life all its own." The chandelier tinkled as she spoke, gently swaying like an enormous uvula.

I should have left then. I should have turned around, gotten in my truck, and driven the two hours back into town. I should have run back to Tommy, begged his forgiveness for getting caught up in Raj's schemes.

I should have done a lot of things.

Instead, I remembered the invoice sheet that Missus Toussaint had signed, the extra zeros she'd added when I'd mentioned that I didn't do house calls. I remembered the credit check that she'd blown out of the water.

And so, I said, "Of course. So, what's been giving you trouble?"

As it turned out, there were quite a few things that required my attention. The back door's lock over-rotated. The bathroom didn't latch half the time. Her liquor cabinet had gotten stuck shut. It was easy work, any handyman could have done it. I didn't mind. It was the first paycheck I'd drawn for a while, and I was happy to let the hours pile up at the rate she'd offered. Denise stayed on my heels the entire time, smiling that enigmatic smile and watching me work.

When we hit the second floor, I glanced down the hall. It was pitch black. Like staring down a yawning chasm. And deep in my heart, I could feel something staring back. A shiver slithered up my spine.

In the darkness, something laughed. I jerked back, heart hammering. My heel missed the drop behind me, and I careened into space. The stairs rushed up to claim me.

Denise's hand flashed out. Immaculately manicured fingers clamped around my wrist like a vice. I stared at the slender woman in shock as she yanked me to my feet without the slightest bit of struggle. She smiled at me. Her teeth were too perfect, too white.

"Honestly, Mister Bhatt," she said, admonishing me like I was a child. "I wasn't expecting such a scaredy-cat."

I swallowed the lump in my throat. "The house settling?"

She chuckled, stepping up onto the next flight. "Come now, Mister Bhatt. There's just one more problem left."

The stairs creaked under my boots. I thought of the money, of the red numbers on my last bank statement. I told myself I believed her.

I ignored the laughter when it came again.

Apparently, Denise's husband had lost his office key before leaving for a work trip abroad, and she wanted to surprise him with a new one when he got back. The door in question was well-fortified. Her husband had sprung for a model that had been in a few locksmith magazines some years back—spool pins, hardened steel core, anti-drill plates behind the face. It was more than enough to stymie any amateur pickers, but I was no amateur. After a morning of dull handiwork, I was looking forward to the challenge.

Denise hovered over me as I knelt before the door and unzipped my tool bag. I could feel her eyes on my back, but I did my best to ignore her. Proper picking needs proper concentration.

"You don't usually do house calls," she said.

I looked askance at her. She smiled down at me like the Cheshire Cat. I nodded.

"So, why did you take this one?"

"The pay's good," I said simply, deciding between two thicknesses of tension rod. "Things have been tight for me recently."

"Because of the money-laundering scandal?" she asked.

I stared silently at a wave rake I knew I wasn't going to use. I didn't respond until I knew my voice would be steady. "You do your research," I said. I settled on a standard pick and got to work, slotting in my tension rod at the bottom of the key well and probing at the pins.

Denise chuckled, musical and sharp.

There's an old urban legend about frogs and hot water. Have you heard it?

It goes like this: if you try to throw a frog into a pot of boiling water, it'll jump out immediately. It can tell that it's in danger and acts to save itself. However, if you put a frog in a pot of *lukewarm* water and slowly raise the temperature to a boil, the frog just sits there like an idiot. Like it doesn't know it's going to die.

In retrospect, I can empathize with the frog. I think I know how he feels.

It's not that he doesn't realize the danger. He sees the pot, the burner, the bastard at the dial. But he also knows they caught him once already.

What other option does he have?

Something thumped again downstairs. I ignored it. I found the tension on pin four, set it above the shear line, kept probing. Just three pins left.

"Honestly, Mister Bhatt," said Denise. "I was lucky to find you. It's so hard to find good help these days."

I squared my shoulders and kept my mouth shut.

The laughter below returned, deep and rumbling. I told myself it was the house settling, no matter how nonsensical that was.

Another thump. This one shook the floor. Denise didn't seem to notice.

Pin one got stuck in a false set. The counter-rotation ended up knocking the others loose again. I started over. Denise rattled on.

"An old house like this," she said, "Well, all sorts of things stop working eventually. Last year it was the heater, the year before that, the lights. This is the first time it's been the locks."

It was then I finally noticed the smell—or maybe it's more that I let myself notice it. Something halfway between copper and burnt hair. Denise reeked of it. The whole house did.

Pin one clicked into place. Number two followed like a dream.

"I was worried at first," Denise crooned, crouching down next to me.

She looked wrong in my periphery. Like the warping at the edges of an old TV, or a Barbie melting on a red-hot stove. "Locksmiths are so in-demand, after all. It's nearly impossible to find one that won't be missed."

I wanted to stop. I knew what was on the other side of that door. But it didn't matter.

My fingers were moving by themselves.

Denise's hot breath tickled my cheek, an inch from my ear. The laughter rose to roar between my ears. Her voice cut through it like a knife. "I wish more men were as desperate as you," she whispered, running a finger down my cheek. "It makes this so much easier."

The last pin clicked into place.

Like it had been waiting.

STATION 99

by Amanda Cecelia Lang

Three weeks after my big brother ditched out on me, I raid his bedroom. Screw him if he thinks he can abandon me in this hell-house with nothing but stale memories and our asshole dad's absentee parenting. I pick Theo's lock with a paperclip and invade the ghost-weed funk of his private domain. Bikini posters, his ghetto blaster, his collection of heavy metal mixtapes. I haul it all down to my basement bedroom and heap it atop the cobwebby boxes of our dead mom's things. I even snag Theo's 13-inch black-and-white TV with the tinfoil bunny-ears.

He warned me if I ever touched it, he'd knock my teeth through my skull. Supposedly, if he tweaks the knobs and bunny-ears just right, he can dial in the Playboy channel. I've personally only ever seen him manage a staticky sitcom. But whatever. I swipe the TV anyway and set it on a cardboard box near the foot of my bed. Its bulky glass-and-steel weight bows the cardboard, but that's cool. Maybe part of me *hopes* it'll collapse and smash to pieces. Just like Theo shattered our whole stupid brotherhood.

I mean, he didn't even say goodbye.

I pop a knob on the television, and a static snowstorm fills the screen. *Click, click, click.* No matter how far I twist the dial, no Playboy channel appears. Not even a bad sitcom. Just static—and I know what happens to morons who stare into staticky TVs. I've seen *Poltergeist*, I'm no scab. I've caught every ghost show, freak show, creep show there is, thanks to our favorite late-night horror hosts.

Svengoolie, Dr. Creep, Elvira, Mistress of the Dark.

Theo and I used to watch them together. Not on this crappy black-and-white heap. But on the TV in the family room, years ago, before Mom went drunk-driving and Dad stopped paying the cable bill. Theo loved the cheesy slashers, and I dug anything with zombies.

Frustrated, I snap his television off. It's getting late, and *I've* still got school tomorrow. My usual lonely routine. I nuke a TV dinner, then crawl into bed with the dismal taste of meatloaf in my mouth. I shed my eyeglasses and sink into the basement's boxy cobweb shadows, staring foggy-eyed out the window. Where's Theo crashing tonight? Somewhere in the city on some rock star wannabe's couch? Some sleazy hotel with his headbanger girlfriend?

Who knows? Dad doesn't care. Wasn't even gonna report Theo missing until I threatened to do it. Then he badmouthed him the whole time—shitty grades, no respect for authority. The cops agreed, runaway punks were a dime a dozen, Theo and his crush were typical rowdy seventeen-year-olds. They said he'd come home when he got hungry enough, or cold enough, or bored enough.

But three weeks, and not even a secret phone call while Dad's working graveyard to tell me he's fine, having a blast. Not so much as a postcard swearing to take me with him one day.

I grit my eyes closed, ignore the pit in my guts until darkness drags me into empty dreams. Painless nothingness.

Feels like a thousand hours later when Theo calls my name.

"Jeremy, dammit, wake up!" His voice crackles.

I grunt into my pillow, pulling myself up from the muck of unconsciousness. Theo brought a lantern, like when we used to camp in the woods behind our house. My bedroom flickers with dull gray light. I fumble for my eyeglasses, but the nightstand's empty.

"Jeremy, it knows us…"

What knows us?

"Dad's gonna pulverize you," I mumble, sitting up, bangs mopping my blurry eyesight. "Where've you been?"

Theo doesn't answer.

I squint at the foot of my bed, at the greasy fog-light of his lantern.

Only, it's not a lantern. His television is on.

Oh balls, I'm dead. "Look, Theo, I'm sorry. You were gone so long…" The excuse fizzles. I squint at the flickering shadow-shapes of my sunken bedroom.

"Theo?"

"Jeremy!" Voice metallic, echoing from the television. *"It gets inside…"*

This has to be a nightmare.

Shadows swirl inside the TV's buzzing light. Blurry-eyed, I practically press my nose to the glass. Static lightning-bolts across the screen, manifesting an eerie smooth-faced creature. No eyes, no mouth, no nose. Just bony limbs and spikey shoulders hunched like an emaciated gargoyle over a white-neon station logo.

Station 99.

The gargoyle-thing tilts its head as if locking that faceless gaze on me.

"Stay tuned for the *Video Macabre*, Jeeerrreeemmmyyy…"

I jerk backwards at the growl of my name. Static rushes the screen, flickering oblivion, and Theo's voice shouts out, crackling, filling with static. *"She's dead… Collette's dead… Blood everywhere…! Jeremy!"*

Before I can unchoke my idiot terror long enough to scream, *What's happening? Where is he? Who the hell is Collette?*—the television sparks and cuts to black.

"Station 99?" Heather Gibson says the next day. We're ditching sixth period, loitering in the ancient tennis courts behind the high school. She flicks a cigarette at me. "You're full of it. Cable channels don't go that high."

"Didn't say it was a cable channel." I lean against the chain link fence, bone-deep exhausted from thinking about this. But I can't stop. "It was something else. A prank. I don't know. But that was Theo's voice. I know it was."

"Maybe he rigged a VCR?"

"There's no VCR. It's just a clunker, some off-brand TV from like the '60s."

Heather scrapes spikey pink bangs aside and lights another menthol. "What about airtime on public access? You said Theo wants to be a rock star."

"A lead singer, yeah." I cough out a laugh. "He's not really any good. But, yeah, maybe that's it."

"Totally. A trippy hardcore opening to some rock video." Heather sucker-punches my arm. "Don't look so gloomy. Your brother's practically famous."

"I guess."

Awkward silence descends. I stare at her steel toe boots. She's cute, in an edgy way. Kinda punk rock and stylish like the girls Theo dates—like girls on MTV. We've hung out off and on since freshman year started, almost three months now. Some days, I get the feeling she likes me, like in *that* way. But I've never made a move. Too afraid to blow it. Afraid if I did, Theo would rib me for shooting above my horizons. Stupid to care what a guy who became a dropout thinks.

"So," Heather says, "who's Collette anyway?"

"His girlfriend, I think."

"You don't know his girlfriend's name?"

I shrug. "He has so many. Anyway, Collette isn't the one he ran away with. That's Amy Sanchez. I think… I think Collette might be Collette Johnson. Some of Theo's friends told me she went missing two nights ago. Her parents went on the evening news and everything."

"Wait, what?" Heather stops smiling. "If she's with Theo, you gotta tell the cops."

"I don't know for sure she's with Theo. It's just something my television said."

"Your television said she's dead. Dude, Jeremy, this is too freaky."

"Maybe I dreamed it."

"Still freaky." Heather flicks her cigarette. "I gotta get to last period."

"That's cool." Wishing I was edgier, wishing I was someone else, I adjust my glasses. Found them under my bed after Theo's television went black. "But hey, will you ask around? See if anyone's heard of Station 99?"

"Or the *Video Macabre*?" Heather does her worst Svengoolie, then clears her throat with an apology. "I'll see what I can find out."

Nine o'clock. Every light in my empty house blazes. My TV dinner congeals on the coffee table in the family room. Should've manned up before sundown. Except, the second I got home, I swore I felt Theo's television in the basement, waiting for me. My bones locked up like picture tubes and steel. All I had the balls for was uneaten meatloaf on the couch, television dark.

Now, I force myself to confront our 32-inch color Zenith. There's a remote, but I think Station 99 prefers dials. I hit the power. Color ignites the screen, a rerun of *Family Ties*. I twist the dial, watching the station numbers flicker past. Without basic cable, ghost-static ices the higher channels, but I keep twisting.

67…73…78…

Heartbeat rioting…81…Static buzzing…83…

The Zenith cycles back to channel 2.

The nine o'clock news.

I'm about to keep going, one more spin around the tilt-o-whirl of madness, but a familiar name stabs my ears.

"…Missing Chester High senior Collette Johnson was discovered this afternoon beneath a city offramp. Police aren't disclosing the nature of her death, but witnesses describe disturbing amounts of blood…*blood everywhere*…"

The newscaster's voice buzzes surreal between my ears.

I stagger into the kitchen and rip the phone off the hook. But who do I call? Heather? Never asked for her number. Dad at his graveyard shift? The cops? And say what? Theo's freaky, possessed television predicted this?

They'll blame him, and Theo didn't do this. No way. *No way.*

I end up pacing the kitchen, back and forth until exhaustion blurs my brain. Need some sleep already.

I approach the basement stairs, chewing my coward lip. The stairwell stretches like a jagged nightmare-throat down to the dank belly of my bedroom. I swipe the light switch. The light bulb hanging at the murky bottom stays murky. Of course it does.

I push my glasses higher. Longer I stare, the more I think I see the dimmest ghost-flicker of gray light down there. Theo? …*Collette?*

"Screw this." I slam the basement door. I'll crash on the couch tonight.

"Jeremy, wake up!"

Theo's voice crackles along the shadow-sticky edges of my mind. I sit up, blinking against murky gray light, and fumble for my glasses on the coffee table.

Only, I'm not on the couch. Where—

My hand knocks my bedside lamp.

It topples but the gray light remains. The light at the foot of my bed.

Theo's television. Glowing with black-and-white smudges, voices buzzing like corpse-flies. *"Blood everywhere…!"*

"Theo? Where are you!" I skitter closer, jam my blurry vision against the screen.

The gargoyle-thing station logo lurks in a test-pattern sea of starless night.

Station 99.

Please stand by…

The words echo my gummy vision.

The gargoyle-thing straightens from its bony crouch.

Static zigzags, and a rolling movie reel fills the screen, counting down…3…2…

The gargoyle-thing reappears.

Looks almost 3D now, live-action. Fish-pale, bald, facing the camera with its featureless face. That fleshy void gapes at me. No mouth, no nose, ribbons of 35mm film blindfold its eyes.

"Welcome back, Jeeerrreeemmmyyy, to Station 99's *Video Macabre!*"

It spreads sharp-nailed hands, and the camera pans out to reveal a haunted graveyard soundstage. Fog-machine mist swirls between balsawood coffins and styrofoam tombstones. Skeletons bask in dangling cardboard moonlight. Just like the campy, low-rent set-ups used by Elvira and Svengoolie.

"Now, lonesome fright fan…" The gargoyle-thing's chin bobs, a muffled meat-puppet voice. "I bring you the blood-soaked conclusion to *Camp Slash-Away,* starring Theo Romero and Amy Sanchez!"

Theo? *Camp Slash-Away?* But I know that movie.

The one about Claw Face, the undead hiker maniac who got mauled by a grizzly while his fellow campers escaped to safety. For revenge, dude shreds every teenager in his woods with steel bear claws.

In a lightning-slash of static, Station 99's graveyard soundstage cuts to a forest. Trees careen past the camera, the shaky perspective of someone running for their life. A smear of log cabins, an archery range. I know this scene! Theo and I watched it a hundred times. This is where the last-camper-standing runs to the boathouse and grabs the harpoon. She's gonna spear Claw Face's eyeball with it—then with a ropy twist and yank of optic nerves, she'll rip out his undead brain! We used to cheer every time. The gross-out effects freaking rock.

But as the camera hard-cuts to the boathouse door slamming open, something's off. The wall of rusty tools and the old rowboat creaking on the water are the same. But the lean-mean camp counselor with the blood-matted blond curls and the shredded Camp Wickery Woods T-shirt isn't any of those things.

She's Amy Sanchez.

Even in black-and-white, I recognize her. My brother's girlfriend. Spikey Joan Jett hair, heavy tear-streaked eyeliner. Instead of yanking the harpoon off the wall, Amy climbs into the rowboat.

"Amy, no!" I shout at the television. "You gotta get the harpoon!"

She doesn't hear me. She grabs an oar, not realizing the boat is roped to the dock, not realizing oars are no match for Claw Face.

A hulking shadow fills the boathouse door.

B-movie moonlight spotlights inky bloodstains on hiking boots and jogging shorts and the meaty scars streaking the maniac's twisted face.

My *brother's* face.

I grip the television, but shit! I jerk away—the metal is red hot!

On screen, Theo surveys the boathouse, steel bear claws glinting from both fists as he steps inside.

He takes his time stalking toward Amy.

"Theo, what the hell?" I cry—and so does Amy.

"Theo!" she begs, trying to wave him off with her oar. "Fuck's sake, snap out of it!"

He catches her oar mid-swing and yanks it away. Violins shriek as he tosses it aside and slashes out with his claws, inches from Amy's horror-struck face.

"Theo, stop!" I shout.

"Jeremy…it knows us!" His ghost voice echoes the airwaves, but his mouth never moves. Flat, expressionless, a meat-puppet silently calling me. He swipes at Amy again. She recoils, screaming, rocking the rowboat. This time his blades graze her chin. Dark wet gashes.

This has to be a joke. A public access *gotcha* he cooked up to torment me for snatching his things.

"Jeremy…" His voice crackles, static-choked inside my spiraling ears. *"Station 99… It gets inside…"*

"Somebody!" Amy turns in a frantic escape-crouch, aiming to dive into the water.

Theo overshadows the rowboat, spreads his arms, and punches both bladed fists into the sides of Amy's throat.

A slash of Technicolor-red paints the screen.

Impossible gore, impossible color. Blood sizzles against the glass. This can't be real, I fumble the coal-hot television knobs, trying to dial back my sanity.

Click, click, click…

Every station is Station 99.

Theo hoists Amy from the boat, clamping her between his claws. She gurgles, gagging up neon blood before slumping into the boat with a grisly splash.

She's dead! *Blood everywhere!* This can't be real!

I punch the on/off button, again, again. Nothing happens.

Theo's television won't turn off!

I tumble off my mattress, skitter toward the outlet, reach for the plug.

"Don't unplug it!" Theo's voice again. At least, I think it's Theo's voice. Strangled vocals, choking on static. *"That's how it gets you…"*

I drop the plug and confront the TV. "What do I do? Theo!"

But the station logo is back. Not black-and-white, but grisly red. The gargoyle-thing hunches over Station 99, watching me without eyes. *Knowing me…*

It twitches, starts to stand.

I back away, letting my crappy eyesight fog the screen.

A feedback screech of laughter fractures the glass, hatching gruesome light into the real world.

High up, the basement window shatters.

A faceless shadow crouches inside.

My bones lock up, icy steel, frozen picture tubes. I watch the nightmare shadow crawl through my window.

"Little help?"

I exhale a ragged, gut-deep breath. "Heather?"

"Sorry about the window." She kicks away teeth of broken glass with her steel-toe boots, then dips her face back in the gap. "Looked you up, saw your light on. Swear I only tapped the glass. To get your attention."

She has it.

"You gonna help me down or what?"

"Oh, yeah." I snap from my daze and scramble over. She spreads her leather jacket across the jagged window edge. Heather freaking Gibson. Any other night this would be the wildest dream come true.

I grip her midnight-cool hands then absorb her weight as she pops down, landing like a punk-rock ninja.

She ruffles the hair out of my eyes. "Did I wake you?"

"No, I was just watching—oh hell, Heather, *look*. Channel 99…"

But Theo's television stands dark.

Dark, silent. Screen uncracked.

"Shit." I fiddle the knobs, but the television stays dead. "I'm not messing with you. Feel, the screen's still hot. I swear, it was just on."

I tell her everything. The faceless gargoyle-thing, *Camp Slash-Away*, Amy and Theo with his dripping steel bear claws. Let it all gush out like a hacked-up jugular. I sound deranged like in the movies, those loopy town drunks nobody ever listens to. But if I don't puke it out, it'll fester inside, and Station 99 is already taking up so much space. It gets inside…

"Holy shit," Heather says when I'm done.

"I get it if you don't believe me."

"No." She stares at her lamplit reflection in Theo's television. "I think I might. Listen, Jeremy, Collette Johnson is dead. Like *really* dead."

"I know." I swallow miserably. "Saw it on the news."

"I asked around," she says. "Station 99 and the *Video Macabre* were dead ends. Not even the geeks at the video store have heard of it. But there *is* something. A girl I know in Collette's art class told me Collette said she needed to get a jacket back from one of her exes. That was two days ago. What if she meant Theo? What if she came here, and Theo intercepted her somehow?"

"No. *No.*" I jerk to my feet, start pacing. "Theo wouldn't do that."

"He's no rock star," Heather says. "What if he decided to be a movie star instead? Only something went wrong. He tried recreating his favorite horror movie, but a death scene got out of hand. After that, maybe things just snowballed."

"You're wrong, you don't know him. Theo wears a hardcore shell, but he'd never hurt anyone."

"You just watched him rip out Amy Sanchez's throat."

"That wasn't him. It was…"

"Who? Claw Face? *Reel Head?*"

"Who?"

"Reel Head." Heather winks at the TV. "The station mascot with the 35mm blindfold? We gotta call it something."

"Yeah, I guess." I swallow thickly. "Theo said it knows us."

"Knows you *how*?"

"Not sure…" The television's square eye gleams at me, reflecting our silhouettes. "Like when you look into it, it looks into you."

Heather folds her arms, tries to conceal a shiver—or a laugh. "Listen, before we get all slippery with theories, we need proof Collette even came here."

"Proof how?"

"Where's Theo's bedroom?"

Upstairs, we pick the lock on Theo's door. Heather hits the light, and I cringe, half-expecting to find Theo sitting in the dark. The room's empty.

"Maybe Collette snuck through the window?" Heather creeps inside, wrinkling her nose at Theo's heavy metal residue. "He just left it like this?"

"Didn't even take his mixtapes." *Station 99 doesn't let you pack…* But I don't say the crazy part out loud. This surreal MTV dream girl, stealing my breath with her friendship and keen, smoky eyes, already thinks I'm bonkers enough.

Atop Theo's dresser, a dust-free square marks the spot his television occupied just two days ago. Nearby, Heather pokes her toe through tangles of dirty laundry and unearths a jacket. The collar sparkles with purple sequins. "Guessing this isn't Theo's?"

I stare at it, vision throbbing with invisible static. "Doesn't mean anything. Maybe it's Amy's or…or… *Dammit!*" I hunch over, fighting a gutful of sick. Not every night your dream girl proves your brother's a psycho killer.

"Hey, it's cool…" She rubs my back. "We're both a little freaked."

"Yeah." I straighten, try to look less spineless. "So, what now? Rat him out to the cops?"

She holds my eyes, doesn't let me flinch. "You think that's why I'm here?"

Isn't it? Our awkward silence again, dreamlike, invading Theo's bedroom like static on a television, growing bigger, buzzing my heartbeat, stealing my voice. Heather bites her lip.

Oh hell, what am I doing? I shadow in and kiss her.

And she kisses me back, I swear she does. Soft but with bite, tastes like cherry lipstick and X-rated daydreams. Except suddenly, she's shoving me away.

I start to apologize for being an idiot, for shooting above my horizon, but she clamps my chin between spikey fingernails and angles my face toward the bedroom window.

Red light sprays the glass, then a splash of blue.

Red, blue, red, blue.

The cops are out there.

Something's happening in the woods behind my house. We watch in eerie silence from Theo's bedroom window, our bleak faces pulsing with a red-blue heartbeat.

Cops use yellow tape to cordon off the trees where Theo and I used to camp. While Heather squeezes my sweaty hand, a coroner's van pulls between the cop cars, stopping slantwise in the weeds. Officers escort the rubber-aproned coroner into the forest, and soon camera flashes ignite the skeletal silhouettes of trees. They're photographing the crime scene. Can't see the body from here, but we both know.

It's Amy Sanchez.

"They're gonna come looking for him," I say. "Any second now, they'll knock on my door. And what do I say? I saw it, Heather. I saw him kill her."

She squeezes my hand. "We tell them the truth."

I cough out a sick laugh. "What truth? That Reel Head made him do it?"

"C'mon." She tugs me back down into the dim throat of my bedroom. She kneels between my bed and the cardboard box propping up Theo's television. Tiny hesitation, then she punches the button. The screen erupts with static. "Looks like it's working now."

"What're you doing?"

"What do you think?" She twists the knob, station after station of snow. With every *click*, my spine shivers, my nerves turn brittle.

"Maybe you should stop," I whisper, like it can't already hear everything we say and think and are.

"Stop?" *Click, click...* "If I witness Station 99, too, we'll have a solid lead. It's gotta be airing from a soundstage somewhere, right?"

Still sounds like she wants to turn my brother in. But that's cool. Feels like I checked out hours ago, just a morbid spectator, watching all this from the comfort of unreality. Heather thinks Station 99 is a place the cops can just *find?* Like with K-9s and SWAT teams?

She wheels through empty channels...*click, click, click*...like Russian roulette.

Nothing happens.

I listen for Theo in the static.

Click, click... A combination lock she just can't crack. *Click-click-click!* Growing hectic—are those faces in the snow? Faceless faces, seeking eyes to fill?

"Stupid thing!" Heather kicks the cardboard box.

The ancient, rotted cardboard crumples, and Theo's television pitches face-first onto my concrete floor.

The screen shatters, sparks, dashes of lightning, a thousand glass pebbles scatter outward like cockroaches.

"Theo!" I cry. A bat-shit reaction, and I know it. Heather backs away, crunching broken glass as I hoist the shattered TV upright.

"God, sorry," she says. "Guess I don't know my own—"

She cuts short.

The television's fine.

We both saw it shatter, can still see the evidence scattered across the floor.

But the television gleams at us, good as new.

The Station 99 logo glows inside phantom static.

Please stand by…

We perch on my bed, knee to trembling knee, waiting for who the hell knows what.

Heather decided we shouldn't stare directly into the Station 99 logo, so now she grips my clammy hand and side-eyes the basement clutter. My dead mom's boxes, shadow-deep, littered with Theo's abandoned things. "This is where you sleep?"

I shrug. "Theo and I used to share a bedroom. He grew out of me, that's all. It's not so bad."

"It's just…" Heather chews her lip.

"Just what?"

"Your whole identity seems buried down here."

I flinch, can't help it. "Sorry I'm such a faceless nobody."

"That's not what I meant."

"Yeah, but you're right. It's like with everyone gone, I don't know who I am."

The static glow ripples across Heather's gorgeous, accepting face. I still can't figure out what she's doing here, middle of the night, with a haunted television and a killer on the loose, manifesting like an apparition I wished for and got.

"You're my dream guy." And she kisses me, lips red velvet. *Heather Gibson kisses me.*

This time, there's no wondering if I overshot.

We clutch each other and go deep, cherry lightning, letting tonight's tension unravel with every kiss. Wild gravity pulls us to the mattress and—

"Welcome back, Jeeerrreeemmmyyy, to the *Video Macabre!*"

Wide-eyed, Heather and I sit slowly upright. The gargoyle-thing with the 35mm blindfold waves hello from Station 99's graveyard soundstage.

"Holy shit." Heather grips my arm.

"Told you."

"Your old pal *Reel Head* here," it says, flesh-mouth twitching. "Back from the shattered grave to continue tonight's dreadful double feature! You just witnessed the throat-gushing new conclusion of *Camp Slash-Away*. Now, which *fright*-mare from the void will thrill you next?"

"Reel Head?" Heather says. "I just made that up."

A wheel of misfortune appears on screen like a game show. A different movie title labels each spiderweb spoke. "Ready for a spin?"

A thrust of Reel Head's bony hand, a black-and-white spiral. *Click, click, click…*

The wheel slows.

The Blob… Chopping Mall… Ghoulies…

Click… click.

Night of the Headbangers.

The one where toxin-dosing zombies infect a rock concert—I used to love this one.

Reel Head claps its pale bony hands. "Ladies and not-so-gentle-men, I give you *Night of the Headbangers*, starring Jeremy Romero and Heather Gibson. Live and *in pieces!*"

"No, *no way*." Heather jerks to her feet. "This is fucked up, Jeremy. Turn it off."

I try, just to show her I tried, punch the on/off button again, again. But it won't turn off. Is this how Theo and his girlfriends felt right before Station 99 took them? An electric sort of inevitability. It crackles in Heather's frantic gray eyes.

She lunges for the power cord, and I grab at her. Theo said to never unplug it, but she does anyway.

Blood-splashed lightning cracks like broken glass, zigzagging the basement. Heather shrieks my name.

She goes light-bright and skeletal.

Everything snaps to white. The air crackles. Thickens. Dims. Ears ringing, head twisting. The Station 99 logo sears my vision, then fades to ghostly afterimages.

All I sense is the concrete floor, a gray blur of movement. *Heather?* My mouth tastes meaty and metallic, coppery, like under-nuked meatloaf.

Somewhere nearby, Heather screams my name.

Lots of people are screaming. Movement. Chaos. Fog. Are the cops here? I blink again, and the patina of static clears. I raise my head.

Not cops. A rock concert.

I see Heather now, up there on the stage in the spotlight, hoisting an electric guitar.

A freak in a shredded concert T-shirt rushes the stage. Rushes Heather! She winds back and swings the guitar like an axe. As his grayscale head explodes in a pulp of neon red, it hits me. Oh hell.

Night of the Headbangers.

My mind bolts upright, sharpens. Rafters line the stage, and spotlights explode electricity, illuminating the toxin-dosed headbangers below. I've seen this scene a hundred times. Soon, a mob of frothing, gnashing zombies will storm the band and trap them backstage. Doesn't end well for them. Only the drummer and a groupie survive...

Because they climb the rafters instead!

No time to freeze. I have to get Heather up there, save her, break us out of this Station 99 hellscape. I shoulder past twitching, foaming headbangers, and scramble onstage. Every metalhead's dream. I angle for Heather, but the lead singer slashes my line of sight.

Alive, uninfected, and swinging his microphone stand like some off-brand Ozzy.

"Theo!" I try to scream it, but my voice froths with static.

But it's really him, and inside I expel a ragged sob.

My brother. Live and in person!

I rush over, reaching for him, barely noticing the toxic-black veins infecting my arms until I shadow Theo's spotlight and take hold.

"Jeremy, what the—" he cries, finally noticing me as I sink my teeth in. "Stop!"

Don't make me do this!

But Station 99 knows us... It gets inside.

And it makes me do it. Like a bony hand lodged gut-deep, protruding up through my throat, flapping my jaw, snapping my frothing undead teeth.

Unable to stop, I chew out my brother's vocal cords with a meaty *rip*.

Blood sprays the black-and-white stage, staining the scenery red.

Blood everywhere.

Theo collapses in a gushing heap, a string-cut puppet. Tendons and meat. Will the cops match his wounds to my dental records? His unbelieving eyes lock on me as I crouch over him, ravenous, *so ravenous*. And I can't stop!

I devour. Even after the light snaps to black behind my big brother's eyes. Gnashing, frothing, screaming inside.

"Jeremy!"

A steel toe boot connects with my head, shatters the picture tube inside.

I pitch sideways, then lift my dripping maw, flesh lodged in my teeth. My toxin-sharp vision shivers, narrows on my brains-and-leather dream girl. Hate for her to see me like this. I wanna wipe my mouth, but my arms don't respond, except to reach for her.

"Snap out of it, Jeremy! You know what Reel Head does." Heather cocks the gore-stained guitar overhead. "Damn it, Jeremy, fight it!"

"I'm sorry!" I try to scream, choking on static, teeth clicking. I can smell my mangled brother, my idol. The same blood infecting my veins pools around his head. I wanna spit.

This isn't who I am.

I shamble to my feet. Heather backs keenly away, wild to swing. Reminds me of the girls who survive gory movies. I hope she's seen this one. Hope she knows what she's gotta do.

"Jeremy? Please! Don't make me!"

Station 99 tightens its hold, bony fist flexing deep.

I try to fight its B-movie toxins—just like Theo tried. Closing in for one last kiss, meat-puppet teeth clicking, voice shouting on mute.

I was Heather Gibson's dream guy, I think as the guitar shatters my vision.

Blood, lightning. Static fills me.

My midnight creep show hard-cuts to black.

(UN)MUTED

Art by Miranda Mundt
Feature by Alli Nesbit

Every chapter of Miranda Mundt's completed Webtoon Originals series, *Muted,* evokes creeping metaphysical dread, the horror of cyclical abuse, and the healing joy of community. The series centers the tale of Camille Severin, a scion of a coven tied to bird-demons by blood magic. Recently, I had the pleasure to sit down with Miranda for a Q&A about her works, her process, and the pieces of ourselves we leave in our characters.

ALLI NESBIT: When you are making *Muted,* are you writing pages of scripts or do you storyboard as you go? Has your process for that evolved with experience?

MIRANDA MUNDT: When *Muted* started, I didn't write scripts. I started writing them when I switched to Webtoon Originals because I wanted to be able to run my thoughts past my editor. I typically make edits between the script and storyboard because the pacing of panels and the flow of the conversation reads differently with the art as opposed to how you can ramble in text forever. Luckily, after the first handful of episodes, my editor was confident that I could go back to my usual process. So, my process has been, more or less, the same ever since.

Pictured left: *Mood Board*

AN: Your use of color is so vibrant, and your character gestures are always incredibly expressive. Did you develop these skills over time, or have they always been a strength?

MM: Color and expression have always been a part of my art, but obviously, they have been refined over time through trial and error. Gestures and expressions have always been incredibly important to me. They are the reasons why I studied animation. As for color, I always worry that my work appears too overpowering and over-saturated, but every time I try to be more subtle, I end up pumping the saturation back up anyway! Haha.

AN: Themes of self-acceptance, generational trauma, and found family are strongly represented in *Muted*. Are there any themes you're looking forward to exploring in your upcoming *Lydia Gray* project?

Pictured top: *Camille Swamp*

MM: I think variations on the themes you mentioned will always be something I'm naturally drawn to, but Lydia's self-acceptance is less about her identity and more about acknowledging how much pain she puts herself through by isolating herself. Camille in *Muted* kept a lot of her emotions buried deep inside, but she still has someone to confide in. Lydia lashes out, but she doesn't have anyone. The trauma in Lydia's story is less generational, but it's still family related.

AN: What inspires your darker works? Where do you draw inspiration from in general?

MM: I feel emotions very intensely. I'm very conflict avoidant. And I don't like being in pain. I think there is a deep emotional catharsis in being able to explore that sort of fear, rage, and pain in a fictional sandbox.

Pictured top left: *Camille Panel 1* **Top right:** *Camille Panel 2*

I'm a big fan of horror movies, shows, and games, but I'm also a fan of musicals and the ways they express intense feelings rather than hiding them or keeping them at surface level. I'm inspired by any media that approaches things with a deep sincerity that I can get lost in. I think that it's a bit of a waste in fiction when something big happens and the emotions are just sort of written off or treated like a joke, like when a character keeps getting knocked down, but they never get a chance to be angry or cry. Why put a character through something if they aren't allowed to actually wrestle with it in some capacity?

There is a feeling I get right in the middle of my ribs when I'm watching or playing something that makes me *feel*. Just a deep ache that almost makes it hard to breathe. Anything that makes me feel that—even for a brief mo-ment—holds a special place in my heart.

Pictured top: *Muted Season Finale Banner* **Bottom:** *Muted Season 2 Banner*

AN: Do you have any getting-down-to-business rituals for when you're starting your work for the day?

MM: Unfortunately, no. Haha. My schedule is wildly unregulated. My best chance is usually if I just jump right into it in hopes of entering a kind of trance state, which does happen on occasion. I'm fortunate that when I do work, I work quickly. So once I actually get into it, I can accomplish a lot. I've been a night owl my whole life, so my most productive times tend to be between 11 p.m. and 3 a.m.

AN: Are you a work-in-silence kind of person or do you listen to music or podcasts?

Pictured above: *Camille Scream*

MM: When I write, I have to write in silence, otherwise that sound will cancel out the characters trying to have a conversation in my head. When I really, really have to focus on something for an intense amount of time, then I tend to find one track to put on repeat. Otherwise, I'm listening to music or a YouTube video essay.

AN: What is your favorite stage of the comic process?

MM: Inking. Color and effects production is always a puzzle, and storyboarding is stressful, but the inking process is pretty peaceful. That's when I know where everything is supposed to go. I just have to clean it up.

AN: Have you ever drawn a scene that surprised you by the time it was finished?

MM: Many times. While working on *Muted,* Athalie and Avaline always surprised me the most. I never intended to have the story shift focus to either of them, but as the story unfolded itself, I realized how much more I wanted to dig into their heads. Many of those episodes are now my favorites.

You can find *Muted* on Webtoon. Also on Webtoon is *LoveBot,* a comic Miranda co-created with her partner, Chase Keels, which is soon returning for it's third season. You can find updates about her new graphic novel project *Welcome Home, Lydia Grey* on her Patreon: patreon.com/anidoodles.

Pictured above: *Lydia*

GOD'S WATCHFUL EYES

by Grace R. Reynolds

Ruslan did not enjoy feeling threadbare strands of muscle stuck between his teeth. It brought him no pleasure to pluck away the soft tissue of a cadaver's mutilated pectoral. Survival was paramount in this Arctic hellscape, however, and he begrudgingly made mincemeat of the rotting body like a long dead fowl. He picked off the scale worms, careful not to pull them too hard lest they tear.

In prison, men warned him of the vague horrors to expect beyond the horizon of evergreens that separated the town from the Laptev Sea. Everyone knew of the Scavengers. The monstrosities who were once human. They were said to scour the rocky beaches in search of something or someone to maul. Seagulls, mollusks, mangled limbs of their comrades in disgrace, discarded like shards of glass along rocks. It didn't matter. All forms of life were equally dispensable in this place. All would serve the remainder of their days under God's watchful eyes.

Ruslan swished the chewy fat around his mouth.

If man was made in God's image, then it could only be true that God, too, was a monster.

Ruslan was not a religious man. He abandoned God in the conventional sense long ago, when the world fell away, crumbling into the sea. When levies gave way to drown millions. When coastlines eroded, taking the cities with them. Sydney, Hong Kong, Los Angeles, Houston, Cape Town,

Venice, Mumbai, Manila—every continent clawed at by salty waters to make way for the slumbering giants below. When the ice caps melted, the monsters of the deep awoke.

An otherworldly screech sounded in the distance, triggering an audible crevasse in an iceberg somewhere offshore. Ruslan shuddered. It reminded him of sirens in the big cities when the threat of a nuclear holocaust occurred daily. The promise of instant obliteration—he could only wish for such a fate now.

The new gods brimmed with insatiable hunger that could only be quelled with blood. Law and order were eradicated for tribal factions to emerge. Punishment indiscriminate. Sacrifice necessary. Criminals, rapists, murderers—the remainder of civilization vowed the worst of themselves would be culled for their perverse worship.

How is it that my offense could warrant such a sentence? So unfair. Deeply cruel. This is, undoubtedly, a mistake to send me to this desolate, violent place. Were they truly unaware of the lengths a lion will go to survive?

Well, violence begets violence. I will leave this place. I will hunt the boy's mother and all of her co-conspirators. I will find them. Slaughter them. Eat them. I will discard their dismembered bodies on the shore for the Scavengers to feed upon. There will be no memorial, no legacies for them. No one remembers the sheep.

In his periphery, a pale-blue Scavenger on all fours approaches the area, hissing with the intent to scare Ruslan off the killed. Ruslan crouched over the macerated torso. This was *his* find. He would not let some half-dead parasite leech from him when his body was still pulpy and pink. Ruslan hissed at the Scavenger with equal measure and scared it off for the time being.

It was impossible not to notice the heavy, foul scent lingering in the air. It permeated all the senses, and the Scavengers were everywhere, like little white maggots writhing on rotting meat in the sun. Frost-nipped bodies wandered aimlessly, blending into the sheets of ice floating behind them. Shriveled black and purple extremities, lacerations infected with clingfish refusing to let go of their latch, forever suckling on their wounds. It was evident for some that their infections grew to mar their skin with barnacles and other parasites, but still they walked on.

Ruslan warily lifted his head. He saw God towering above them with its moss-green gelatinous body. There were innumerable eyes on its head, and Ruslan's focus followed the large, yellow orbs. The irises swiveled with the jerk of every spastic movement, ever watchful, always lusting for its next meal.

As God opened its mouth to continue feeding, acidic saliva sloughed the skin of those directly beneath. A collective wretch thrummed across the beach. A prayer, perhaps, or a hymnal in preparation for the Eucharist. Some of the Scavengers fell to their knees. Others genuflected. There would be no bread for the sacrament, no cruet set of brine and wine. Their dry, cracked lips became the rim of their chalice to receive communion.

One by one, God ingested a select few to satiate its appetite. Rows of teeth shredded them, a rain shower of blood and skin, like discarded ribbons falling from the sky into the hungry mouths of the Scavengers and their brethren below. Nourishment was scarce on the Laptev Sea, but God would always provide.

Ruslan curled into a ball to protect his body from a gust of snow and ice. He glanced up again, watching their abominable God. Sulfur blasted out of its orifices, popping pustules of skin riddled with abscesses.

Ruslan had to escape the shoreline. Find his way to another settlement in the interior of the country. Adopt a new name, clean his slate, and forget the madness that brought him here.

The midday sun rose ever higher in the sky. Ruslan's back was raw and sun-blistered now. He grasped his neck, willing himself not to scream as his sanity hung in the balance. Ruslan would not last much longer in these conditions, but he must persevere. He did not want to become a Scavenger, but with every swallow of human flesh he felt the change shifting within. The pale-blue tint of his fingers had spread to his wrists now. It would not be long until he, too, lost himself in worship.

Noxious gas spewed droplets into the sky as God undulated its bloated form. They trickled down its mucous coating, and the eyes shook once more. They quickly zeroed in on Ruslan, and God bellowed out for all to look upon his shrinking form.

They were aware of him now. Ruslan could only mutter curses under his breath, struggling to think of what to do next. As the Scavengers continued to writhe with anticipation, Ruslan saw a dead hand poking through the bottom of a mound of decaying limbs. A sharpened length of driftwood held tight in its clutch.

There was no time to think, no time to plan. Ruslan sprinted. He leaped over skeletons and half-picked carcasses, pushing God's drifting, mindless followers out of the way. Ruslan yanked the driftwood from the clutch of death, only to immediately spin around and thrust it into the eye of a Scavenger behind him. Blood splattered Ruslan's face as he pulled the spike out of the Scavenger's eye socket, ignoring the gobbets of brain matter dangling on its edges.

Adrenaline overcame him, and Ruslan fought the hoard of Scavengers off one by one. With every inch he made toward the copse of evergreens beyond, more cannibals shifted their focus to him. Together they moved as one, a singular body of gangrenous limbs kicking, scratching, desperate and hungry.

Ruslan let out a howl as nails dug into his calves. Fingers hooked inside his cheeks and pressed his eyes to the point he thought they would explode. Ruslan's screams were muffled by skin slapping against him like the rise and fall of waves. His body was now lost somewhere among the hundreds carrying him back to the sea. With no way to flex his arms or legs free from the mass, all Ruslan could do was reflect back on his perceived heroism at the Magazin.

A ripped plastic bag. Spilled cans on the linoleum floor. Hands on shoulders. Cheek to metal shelves. Police storm the narrow doorway of the Magazin. The barrel of my Glock pointed at the back of the teenage boy's head. My fingers hovering over the trigger, ready to fire. Handcuffs. A screaming mother. An arrested son.

Ruslan was told they were to expose, convict, and sentence the worst of themselves. Was petty theft not indicative of immoral character? Ruslan was the one who stopped the boy; he was the one that sent another criminal, a *true* criminal, to Laptev's shores.

Ruslan remembered the boy's mother, how she screamed at him until her face turned blue. He would not feign sympathy, however. Boys are supposed to grow up to be responsible, law-abiding men led by a strong moral compass. If their family was starving, where was his father, and if his father was not there, then why was the mother or the boy not adequately providing for their family?

In Ruslan's mind, the boy had stolen twice over: the first from the Magazin, the second from his own family through his lapse in judgment that resulted in his death sentence. Now the boy's family was without a potential source of income. *Yes, the boy was selfish*, Ruslan told himself. His family would surely die of starvation now. That would make him a murderer most assuredly, no doubt having earned his rightful place among God's laymen.

Ruslan's body rose. The Scavengers swelled with desire to be near the impending flood of gristle and viscera, pushing him higher up their barbaric tower of Babel. He looked at their faces. There were so many, their features cloistered in clam shells and worms. Their eyes hollow craters for crabs and sand fleas. Together they retched once more, drowning out the sound of the birds cawing high above in the sea air.

So many faces. His face—the boy to his right—was strange and familiar. It was then that Ruslan recognized the boy as the one he threatened to shoot at the Magazin.

They were in conflict with one another yet again, though this time Ruslan was the sacrificial lamb and the boy was the oath keeper. *Punishment indiscriminate. Sacrifice necessary.* Together they were the paradox of innocence and guilt. The culmination of decisions made through a utilitarianist lens whose new world diocese of malice was never interested in justice.

Ruslan thought back to the Magazin, the look of terror in the boy's eyes. Ruslan knew where the boy was going; he knew the boy would die out here and didn't care. He didn't have to, because until now, until he was punished for a crime, this sort of thing didn't affect him.

Criminal. That was all Ruslan ever saw the boy as, but the world disagreed. To the world, Ruslan was the criminal. A thief. A murderer. He was not heralded as a hero, as Ruslan thought he should have been. He was a vilified nobody.

There will be no memorial, no legacy for me.

The reality of his error washed over him like a tidal wave, drowning him in a stream of salty tears. He sobbed and cried out to the boy.

"I'm sorry! I'm so very sorry! Please forgive me! Help me leave this place, and I will take you back to your mother! We can forget all this ever happened! God, please forgive me!"

As God extended its mandible to reach him, Ruslan stared at rows of silver serrated teeth. They spun like the blade of a table saw, waiting to slice through him. He looked back into the boy's eyes, or where they should have been, but was met with silence. There was no offering of repentance. There would be no forgiveness, no forgetting.

Ruslan was overcome with fear. He was enraged. All his life, Ruslan thought of himself as a lion, the kind of man who would not bend to the wills of sheep! He snapped his neck back toward the boy and spat,

"I should have shot you! Let your body bleed out in front of your poor excuse of a mother! You piece of shit, you cretin! *You* deserved this, not me!"

The hoard pushed Ruslan into God's chamber, placing him on its tongue like a sacramental wafer. He was just a face, a face of many faces stitched together with needle and twine to create a wet blanket of flesh and bone, antagonism and barbarism cured. Ruslan was but another son whose deliverance would stave off another day of terror by their merciless God.

GHOUL

by Victoria Nations

The human stood at the mouth of the alley, staring at Ghoul. She would be a silhouette to another human, with the low sun throwing rays from behind her. Shadows from the tall buildings had already crept most of the way across the alley. But Ghoul saw the fall of her rust-colored hair against her pale cheeks and the dark blue underlayer that was nearly the same color as her bristly coat. Her boots and jeans marked her as different from the suited commuters who passed on the sidewalk. The human's gaze was direct, could have been seen as aggressive, but the submissive tilt of her head signaled that she meant Ghoul no harm.

"Are you okay?" The woman held her arm out towards the squatting Ghoul. "Do you need help?"

Ghoul stayed still, willing the human to lose interest and wander off. Worse creatures than Ghoul frequented the alley, and it was best if the woman not stick around to find out.

"I'm Katie. I work a couple blocks down. Near the tunnels."

The human's arm had dropped a bit, but she kept chattering. Her soft, lilting words made Ghoul's shoulders want to relax.

"I walk past here every day. Well, not every day. Just on days I work. Tonight, I was walking faster because of the rain, and I thought about you."

Ghoul held her squat. The lower vantage point felt safer in the human city, where the trees stood alone. If she had a canopy of branches above her, she would scramble up and away from this encounter. The human would never find her.

With her bony knees close by her head and her palms planted on the asphalt, she was ready to spring into the air if the human moved closer.

"See, I usually walk in the tunnels, especially when it rains, but they were closed tonight. Crime tape. And…" The human paused to squint into the alley, as if she couldn't quite see Ghoul in the fractured light. "I usually see you in those tunnels, the ones near my shop, and I wanted to make sure you were okay. There was blood."

The last part was rushed and breathless, so quiet a human would have strained to hear what she said. But Ghoul heard the low warbling behind the human's words. It was almost a mewling. The human was bright-eyed, like the young ones in the trees, and just as vulnerable.

Ghoul shifted from foot to foot, hands now clasping her ankles. She knew why the tunnel was closed. She touched her matted hair that was twisted into bloody dreadlocks.

The human studied Ghoul's face and glittering eyes. "Anyway, I thought you might be cold outside the tunnels, with the rain and all." She removed her coat and placed it on the ground. She rocked back on her heels for a moment, and when Ghoul didn't come forward, she ducked her head and hurried off, her arms wrapped around herself.

Ghoul tracked the human's steps, artless as her younger sisters, as they faded into the dark, certain such a creature would be killed by the predators that roamed this territory.

Despite Ghoul's camouflage, the human was able to track her while she foraged in the tunnels beneath the city. Ghoul didn't look like a threat while hunched on the floor or leaning against the wall. She was small, and her naked limbs were slender. She just hid in the shadows, dark eyes gleaming behind her shaggy hair. The many humans that took shelter in the tunnels paid her no mind.

Ghoul crouched in the shadows as the last of the commuters passed, their eyes fixed forward, ignoring the bodies that slept along the tiled walls. One by one, the small shops along the tunnel closed for the night, and the humans dwindled until only those with guarded walks and suspicious eyes braved the remaining night. These were the ones Ghoul followed. Hearing their footfalls echo in the empty corridors made her nostrils flare with anticipation.

The night prior, a man in a raggedy coat made his way through the tunnel, his glassy eyes staring down at his feet as if willing his wobbling steps into a straight line. Despite his best efforts, he lurched side to side. His swaying made his confusion worse, and he searched the blank walls as if looking for a way out, he saw a man quickly approaching him. The man's face brightened when the man reached out with thick arms and bundled him into a tight embrace. Both men ignored the waif who crept closer as they wrestled. They enjoyed a moment of intimacy before the predator struck.

A guttural yell echoed, followed by the sounds of tussling and the slap of feet on the tiled floor. Gurgles thrummed against the walls, but they tamped down quickly. By the time Ghoul's thin form rose from the corner, the wet smacks of the dead man's spasming arms had stilled. The man's arms were tangled, and his throat was cut and gaping. Half-moons of blood traced the ground where he had kicked his legs. His face was slack, his mouth loose and open, pressed against the bloody floor. A meaty tang of blood and adrenaline wafted up from his corpse and was carried to the nose of Ghoul on a breeze.

The attacker left the body where it lay, and Ghoul had him all to herself.

She scrambled to him, all knobby legs and pale monkey arms, and slurped his blood from the ground. It was rare she got so fresh a kill. Ghoul threw her head back, hair splattering her back with blood. The stripes would help conceal her as she moved between shadows.

She relished the cooling blood against her face, coating her body and legs. The man did not flinch as she pulled a gobbet of flesh from his neck and chewed it enthusiastically.

Katie returned a week later and walked farther into the alley. Ghoul watched from her den of pallets and cardboard. The human woman stepped carefully around the jumbled piles of trash and debris, her eyes searching for movement.

"Hello? I'm not sure if you remember, but I'm Katie. I thought I'd come by and see how you're doing."

Her high voice echoed between the building walls, a clarion to things that might hunt her. This silly human didn't seem to understand. An alley where the bodies disappeared afterwards was especially appealing to the more sinister predators in the area. No one ever found the bodies stacked around her den, the bones picked clean, but predators will hunt where they can corner their prey.

Ghoul stood on two feet and walked toward Katie, her practiced gait meant to mimic a human teenager. Her long shirt hung over her bony legs, and filth streaked her face and arms.

Katie's human face crumpled with worry.

Ghoul and her sisters could never camouflage the black eyes that marked them. It mattered less in the forest, but Ghoul had to adapt when she moved into the city. She had to evolve.

"You look cold." Worry was clear in the human's voice. "You didn't like the coat?"

Ghoul looked to a nearby garbage pile, to where she had discarded the girl's gift.

"I don't want you to be cold." The human's voice was wheedling again.

Ghoul went to the pile, picked up the coat, and put it on, her eyes never leaving Katie's.

Katie beamed at Ghoul. She was as mercurial as a young one who mourned their prey, then delighted in ripping it to bits.

The coat hung to Ghoul's knees and was quite warm. The fabric felt soft against her grimy skin. The shirt had been a concession, camouflage to avoid detection in the human-filled city, but the coat felt like too much, too…human.

Ghoul preferred not to be tied to anything other than her hunting sisters in the forest. Together, they could decimate a body and flock back to the trees in a few hours. They draped themselves with the flesh of their prey and fashioned their hair into trinkets. Most humans dismissed them as myth, but there were those who looked for them, who ventured deep into the wilderness and became injured or lost. Tales of arboreal women descending to carry off the dead left out how they picked the bodies clean and scattered the bones.

Ghouls had no words, only grunts, groans, and wails. They called to each other as they clambered through the trees, trusting the front to lead them, trusting each other to gather the feast. Ghoul's sisters wouldn't beam, show all their teeth like this human, but they would take care of each other when needed.

Ghoul remembered. She had adapted. She had evolved.

She didn't need the coat to stay warm, but she kept it on. The happy murmurs of the human sounded the same as her sisters' cooing.

Ghoul sat away from the golden bands of sunlight that stretched across the alley. The rays illuminated a sticky pool of drying blood and drag marks that extended back into the alley to where she'd stashed the body for a nighttime feeding. The thick man had left it, confident his kill would disappear. He moved through the areas where Ghoul scavenged, quietly and with certainty, and he visited the mouth of the alleyway often. His pleasure seemed to grow each time he found it empty.

Ghoul would get lazy if he continued to range through her territory. A full belly and the sunlight were already making her sleepy.

The humans lived in cities and rarely ventured into the forest like they had in her mother's time. Back then, her sisters had to search far and wide for prey, giving their meager meals to the young one's first. Ghoul had left them, her gaunt frame shaking with hunger, determined to find prey on her own. She'd walked until she found a human, dead and abandoned, slumped against a building. She'd fed until she was bursting. No humans were around to scare her off her meal, and no sisters were around, forcing her to share. She'd decided to stay because food was plentiful, and she remained alone because it would be impossible to move through the city in flocks.

To the humans, she was just another feral being who lived on the streets, and she moved among them with ease. True predators moved among the humans too, but these predators were different from the bears and big cats of the forest. They hated their prey, and they killed not for food, but for sadistic enjoyment. There was no honor in what they did. No respect for the dead.

They just left their prey lying there, mutilated and uneaten.

Even the rare ones who took trophies only took small tidbits. The human predators were useful, but their prey often went to waste. There was too much left over for only her to eat, no sisters to share in the kill.

She licked the blood from her hands and wiped them off in her hair, dreamily tightening its coils. The pleasant aromas of spilled blood and human scent mixing with her own inside the coat reminded her of sleeping with her sisters after a meal.

Lost in memory, she nearly missed the intruder.

The coarse hair on Ghoul's back stood on end as she let out a guttural, ratcheting cry that boomed throughout the alley. The startled human jumped as Ghoul leapt at them, her hairy back arched and her face a twisted mask of fury.

"It's me!" the human shouted. "It's Katie!"

Ignoring the human's words, Ghoul scuttled forward, teeth bared, her grinding call rumbling from her chest.

Katie stumbled back, putting distance between herself and Ghoul's raging body that twisted into monstrous angles, barely contained by the splitting coat. Katie fell to her knees, her body flattened in supplication. She raised a trembling hand like before, smooth like Ghoul's young sisters, the pad not yet callused, the claws too short to drag prey up into the branches. Tangles of blue and rust hid her face, but Ghoul knew tears were in her eyes, hot and terrified, like any young one begging for comfort.

Ghoul squatted and quieted her growl to a pant. Her arm trembled as she reached out, like it did whenever she climbed into the treetops, hot blood thundering between her ears. Katie's fingers worked against Ghoul's until they were no longer hooked in, an attack position meant for gouging out eyeballs and ripping out tongues. The human's skin was soft and downy, so unlike Ghoul's course hair. But their slender limbs felt the same.

Katie reached out to touch Ghoul's face, but Ghoul shied away, then retreated to her den. She did not bother to hide its location this time, just crouched there in the open and stared at Katie until she left.

The autumn rains came back, and to keep warm, Ghoul curled into the fetal position inside the human's coat. She'd piled trash bags around her den to create a protective barrier against the coming winter, which made the air inside the enclosed nest hot from her body heat and breath.

The den was cozier than what she'd built in the forest. The human buildings stood against the wind better than the trees, which swayed and whipped when the winter storms came, plus their remains didn't rot like the branches she used to gather. She was warm enough with only herself, her nest nearly complete. It would be easy to tell herself she didn't need her sisters. Had she still lived in the forest, they would still be gathering, still preparing for the winter. They'd crawl into a heap of bodies, bony arms and legs entangled atop a nest of prickly pine needles, and still, they would shiver. The sticky smell of resin and warm bodies would be cloying, nearly overwhelming, by the time winter finally broke. If they hunted fresh creatures, the humans would surely smell their nest in the dry, cold air and avoid it. Ghoul never worried that her den would be found in the city, since here, everything smelled of humans and rotting things already.

"Hello? It's me again, Katie."

Ghoul shifted to look out through the slits she'd left between the piles of garbage. The human stood at the mouth of the alley, looking around to see if Ghoul was there.

"It must be cold out here, having rained all night." The human smiled sheepishly, her eyes searching the piles of trash where she'd seen Ghoul emerge from before. The warble was in her voice again. "You could come back with me to the shop. It's warm there. I can get you something to eat."

The human watched for movement, then dropped to the ground. She squatted and relaxed her posture, purposely looking small and non-threatening, mimicking the stance that had let them touch before.

Ghoul gaped at the kneeling Katie, this false sister of the city. Katie found Ghoul's eyes between the bags and smiled. Vulnerable. Like a fawn grazing thoughtlessly at the edge of a meadow, its slender neck stretched as if offering to have it torn out.

If Ghoul were the human's sister, she'd have taught her to perch high and hide in the trees. She'd have counseled her to never climb down until she was fast enough to run from the beasts, and even then, only with the others.

But there were no trees here. Only beasts.

"Hey girl," the thick man said, and Ghoul tensed.

Katie swore under her breath. She might have been naïve to the ways of the forest, but she was still a city girl, and she knew she'd let her situational awareness slip. She stood and faced the man who blocked the alley opening. She refused to look startled. Ghoul would have been proud of Katie's grit, had the girl not first put herself in so much danger.

The thick man's eyes were amused. They smiled as he searched the alley for any possible witnesses.

"Imagine my luck, finding you alone."

The thick man had brought Ghoul many meals. Her den was stocked for the winter with the bodies he'd left on her doorstep. Such a predator would no doubt kill a young one like Katie with hardly a thought.

Ghoul had adapted to the city, to denning alone.

She had evolved.

But she would still protect her flock.

Ghoul threw off her human clothes before she charged the man. Coarse hair stood up like spines from the prominent ridge down her back, doubling her girth. She snarled as she launched herself at him, her thin legs clamping him like a vice when she landed, her fingers scrabbling for his eyes.

The thick man screamed and contorted his body, trying to throw her off, but Ghoul clung tight the same way she would when gripping a body that she'd scavenged with her sisters, fighting for her piece. Her teeth, built for ripping meat from the bone, were just as effective when the prey was still alive.

Katie stood frozen as Ghoul fell upon him, slurping at the blood spurting from his neck. Katie's eyes, wide with wonder and fear, were the last thing Ghoul saw before burrowing into flesh. All was a red sheen while she scrabbled at his arms, skin curling under her claws, while she smacked and swallowed until the blood slowed to a trickle and the thick man stopped kicking. Gore dripped down her cheeks when she finally looked up.

The young human had bravely stood her ground, even watched as Ghoul did her hideous work. She learned how to take down the beasts that threatened her, and she did so without looking away.

Ghoul left the meat and crawled to Katie, her body so low to the ground, the wet ropes of her hair dragged along the pavement. The young one's eyes blazed in her pale face, and Ghoul called out to her, a low trill of notes, a song of victory and kinship.

Katie yodeled back, a halting imitation, but so similar they could be sisters.

DARK MATTER PRESENTS

MONSTER
LAIRS

A DARK FANTASY
HORROR ANTHOLOGY

EDITED BY ANNA MADDEN

LIZARD MAN

by Polly Hall

I didn't want to look, but I knew it was him.

Too many nights I had wondered how long he would live alone outside, wearing hardly any clothes, even when the earth turned iron-hard with frost. His familiar voice crackled where he rarely held conversation and seemed to echo like the rooks or jackdaws calling at nightfall. Words and small talk were about as useful to the Lizard Man as a knitted bucket. That's what we called him, *Lizard Man*, on account of his skin being patterned all over with scale-like tattoos. They had faded over the years, and by some reckoning, he must've been younger than I imagined. Living rough had given him a gnarled, woody appearance.

I watched a car disappear as it turned right at the end of the track, dust rising up to momentarily obscure the hedges and trees. A buzzard appeared overhead and skimmed the tops of the ash trees, letting out a lonely cry. I rode my bike back to the farm and let myself in the back door. Ma was up to her elbows in feathers, breasting out pigeons for our tea. Sal, the old dog, freeze-framed in an eager pose, sat looking hopeful for any spare bit of meat. She turned and wagged her tail at me before resuming her position by Ma's legs.

"What you been up to son?" Ma spoke with her back turned away, but my face reddened as if she were looking straight at me, reading my thoughts. She pulled back the feathers and skin, then sliced through another pigeon breast, dropping the floppy carcass into a bowl on the worktop. Sal shook her fur coat and let out a soft whine.

"Just out on my bike," I mumbled, still breathless from racing back, wanting her to ask me more questions, wanting her to slice out the truth like she did with her knife on those dead pigeon carcasses.

"Good lad. Go fetch me some beans from the garden, will you?" Her hair was tied up in a loose tangle atop her head, exposing the dark-blue discoloration on the back of her neck, just above the collar. Her apron ties were coming loose behind her back, and I noticed how the hem of her skirt was uneven where the fabric had hitched up over her behind.

I scraped my chair back across the slate floor and stood. Sal yapped, impatient for attention, still looking up at Ma, eager for any morsel that might magically appear. Ma glanced over her shoulder at me as I ruffled Sal's fur around her collar and pulled back her ears to feel the warm, silky lining between my fingers.

"Ma," I said. "Do you remember the Lizard Man?"

Ma paused for a moment as if catching her breath, hands held over the sink. She twisted round again to look at me.

"The Lizard Man?"

"Yeah, I think he's—' I was interrupted by a loud knock on the door that made both Ma and myself jump. People rarely knocked when they visited; they just walked straight in, round the back. But the knock was at the front of the house. I couldn't remember the last time I'd even entered through that door. Sticky cobwebs had formed a skin across the wooden frame there, and ivy had crept up like a leafy serpent to conceal much of the door.

Ma raised her blood-flecked hands above the sink as if to excuse herself from answering the door. "Be a love, will you?"

I trudged to the door, and Sal followed at my heels, yapping with excitement, distracted momentarily from food. As I got close to the cobweb-infested entrance, I could see through the frosted glass window in the door the outline of a large man in a hat. The sunlight silhouetted his head and broad shoulders. Sal yapped as I unlocked the door, the bolt stiff where the heat of many summers and the damp of many winters had made the wood warp and move as if it were still rooted and alive.

I tugged at the door and Sal lurched forward through the gap, sniffing around the man's legs. He was dressed in a light-colored suit, with a white shirt, and linen trousers. He wore a trilby and had the kind of tan you only acquire from leisurely watching boats chug down a jungle river. He looked familiar, but it was possible that he just reminded me of an actor on the telly. Sal sniffed his shoes with a passion even I found embarrassing.

"May I speak with Mrs. Pritchard?" the man asked. His accent was unmistakably American. He removed his hat, held it against his chest, and smiled. 'Is she home today?' He was polite, but I sensed urgency in his voice.

It was odd hearing Ma's name formally announced. *Mrs. Pritchard.* It had been an age since I'd heard her addressed this way. Everyone just called her "Ma." I turned to fetch her but was surprised to see her already standing behind me. She wiped her hands on a tea towel, straightened her skirt, and pushed back her fringe.

"I'm Mrs. Pritchard. How may I help you?" She put on a fake posh accent that she always used when on the telephone or when she was in the company of strangers for the first time. I felt unnerved when she behaved like that, talking through her lipstick and straightening her back. She was like an imposter wearing someone else's skin.

The man nodded a greeting. "I'm Detective James," he said. "I've taken over for Detective White. I believe you knew him as Bobby." He reached into his breast pocket and flashed his ID. Looking up at him was like peering up at a tall monument carved from marble.

Ma's face slackened, and I thought she was going to faint.

"Is he…? Have you…?" her sentences were unfinished, but the man seemed to understand her whispered half-questions.

"Mrs. Pritchard, perhaps it's best if I come inside."

Years ago, back when I was only nine, Ma used to hire men to help around the farm. One of the men, Dougie, even lived with us for a while. He was big with soft edges and ancestral strength, reminded me a lot of a bull. I once saw him lift a car with his bare hands and hold it up like he was lifting a child. I liked Dougie. I laughed whenever he made shadow puppets on the barn walls: a rabbit with big ears, a dog with its tongue lolling, an elephant, a tortoise.

There was also a girl called Bridget who said she was *traveling*. She arrived in the middle of the night with just a knapsack and needed somewhere to stay. Her hair was so blonde it was almost white. She reminded me of a dolly, but she could lift bales of hay and sacks of spuds with ease. And she used to cook me pancakes and twirl honey from a spoon. I missed Bridget after she left. She taught me words like *kartoffel* and *gesundheit,* but Ma said I wasn't to go repeating them in front of the others.

Then there were the others I didn't warm to, like slinky Jeff, who would creep about at night, making the floorboards creak in the worst of ways. I was convinced he was a spy or a peeping Tom but I was only a kid, so no one believed me. Then there was old Mr Shawshank who never cut his fingernails and always smelled of mold and rotting dung. Ma would scrunch up her nose whenever she came near him, and at meals, he would chomp noisily, mouth opening and closing like a dustcart.

But it was the Lizard Man who I remember best. He was slight in frame, with long, muscular limbs, and he had big blue eyes like Ma's. His head was bald and smooth, and he seemed to not have any body hair at all. Most of the time he wore no clothes, but he'd cover up his privates with a small loin cloth if he was around company. He never seemed to get cold. He would often sit motionless and gaze at some random point in the distance without blinking. On days when the heat was too much for most people, he'd lay out in the sun and absorb the rays. He came and went often, and every time he disappeared, I felt a pang of loss, like a tree might feel after shedding its final leaf before winter.

I imagined he had come from Scotland, but in reality, he had grown up on an island in the Pacific, the name of which I can't recall. Most of the villagers knew of him, and they gave him a wide berth when possible. Ma always said that we had to make the most of other folk no matter their differences, because they were our greatest teachers.

He must've been old a long time before he came to the village, because his skin was wrinkled and faded, marked with dark blues and greens. Tattoos covered him from his neck to his feet, scaly patterns that made him look like a human/reptile hybrid. When he first came to the farm, I ran and hid behind the barn, where I watched him step barefoot across the yard and peer oddly into the windows of our home. He crept silently along the perimeter and disappeared round back. That's when I heard Ma's voice and hushed, excitable conversation.

He never really stayed with us inside the house. He preferred to sleep in the woods. But he was around for a long time. He'd bring Ma rabbits he'd caught and fruit he'd harvested from the hedgerows in exchange for a cooked meal. Sometimes he wouldn't turn up until dark, but he always returned the bowls or mugs she left out for him. I saw Slinky Jeff throw a rock at him once when he thought no one was watching.

I don't ever remember Lizard Man smiling, but I knew in my bones that he was as content as a man could be. He seemed happy in his skin. I would stare at his bare legs and think about touching the intricate patterns tattooed on them. I would wonder about the colors in the rain. Did they smear? One time, I drew all over my arms and legs with a pen. Ma scolded me and made me scrub it off until my skin stung, raw and red. She gave me a look like I'd shamed her, and in my confusion, I shouted at her, told her she loved the Lizard Man more than she loved me. She just looked pained and sent me to bed.

One night, not long before the Lizard Man disappeared, I heard voices outside my bedroom window. One voice was Ma's, and the other was the Lizard Man's. The high pitch of his voice was unmistakable.

"…Won't let you tell him…"

"…Not fair on the boy…"

"…Flesh and blood…"

After that night, things started going missing. Neighbors would complain that their windows had been tampered with, that items had been stolen. Nothing was ever taken from our house, but we didn't own anything of much value either. Plus, Sal would bark if anyone came near the house, and the geese were good at chasing off intruders. After a few meetings between the villagers, suspicions grew. Whispers spread like weeds.

Mrs. Pritchard's been entertaining layabouts, vagrants, ne'er-do-gooders.

Mrs. Pritchard is one of them.

Mrs. Pritchard harbors spies.

I thought of Bridget, with her sweet humor and generous hugs, and Dougie, with his slow, gentle ways. But I knew in my heart who they were really talking about: the Lizard Man.

Ma said it was because they didn't know any better. It was easier to judge than to accept. She told me how when we first moved to the village, we were ignored. The only ones who helped us out and treated us like real people were the odd strangers who visited the farm.

That night I heard the Lizard Man outside my bedroom window with Ma turned out to be the last I'd see or hear of him. Still empty bowls continued to show up on the windowsill, the occasional rabbit was still strung from the door frame, and random piles of nuts and berries still gathered by our gate. Ma never hired any more help. She decided we could manage on our own. And I suppose we did. She kept a few sheep, and we trundled on as best we could.

There were times when I thought I'd seen a blue-green pattern shift between the trees or hear that high-pitched wail on the wind. But it wasn't until that day when I saw his body, curled up and silent as a rock, that I questioned who the monsters really were. He was laid in a sort of burrow, next to a large oak. His skin was covered with dead leaves and ferns, and flecks of soil obscured the intricate patterns, making him blend seamlessly into the ground. He could have been sleeping, so I left him alone. I did not want to disturb him, and I was afraid that if he awoke, he would simply run away.

But it was Ma's heavy hand on my shoulder after that new detective left, asking if she could have a few moments to talk with me, when I realized that the worst monsters lived inside of me and not out there in the woods.

Dark Matter
Presents
THE BLEED

DEVIL CHILD

by Kay Hanifen

"You were born under a bad sign," Mother once said. "I should have known then, when the pain started, that you'd be nothing but misery." She would comb my hair, braid it into dual pigtails, her hands rough and tugging so hard it hurt. I'm not sure why she bothered. Why she played at making house. We both knew she abhorred me.

Abomination.

Devil child.

Monster.

And yet she braided my hair, tried to hide the budding horns on my forehead as though, with just the right bit of magic, she could also conceal my cloven hooves, leathery wings, and leonine face. As though I was her daughter and not a punishment for her sins.

She told me the story countless times. Her sacrifice. Mother the martyr who laid with the devil so that the rest of the family would survive the winter. A bargain struck. Their lives for the temporary use of her womb. But her husband was horrified and left by spring, their children in tow. Leaving us alone. Hoping we'd starve or freeze or die in a thousand other ways when abandoned in the woods. She loved to tell me the story of how she gave birth alone in this very shack. How she thought she would die. How the shock nearly killed her when she finally saw the creature that had been inhabiting her womb as it blindly tried to crawl up to her and suckle her breasts. She should have died, and I never should have existed. Through the infernal machinations of my father, though, we survived.

When my horns grew too big to hide behind my thinning hair, she gave up trying to conceal them with braids. Instead, she tried to saw them off. I woke one morning with my hands, feet, and even wings tied to my bed. She straddled me, a saw in one hand, and pressed my head down with the other. And then she cut into them.

The agony was like cutting off a limb. I screamed, bucking, and kicking as she struggled to saw the bones from my forehead. "Shut up!" she shouted, punching me in the face. My head snapped back in shock, and she took advantage of my stunned state to finish with the first horn.

I was silent for the second. It hurt just as much as the first, but I didn't dare raise her ire again for fear that she would finally decide she'd had enough of me and saw off my head while she's at it. Once she was done, she retrieved a looking glass and held it in front of my face with a smile. "There. Isn't that better?"

Blood and bone marrow trickled down my face, and everything was a mess of snot and tears. I looked worse than if she had just let me keep the horns, but still I said, "Yes, Mother."

She pressed a rare, tender kiss to my forehead, and I did my best not to sob at the burning pain her lips caused. "My good little girl."

The horns grew back a week later, but Mother didn't bother trying a second time to remove them.

Mother is dead. She's been dead for a time now, her purpose apparently served. My father's magic no longer sustained her. I buried her in the back-yard underneath her favorite tree. She may not have liked me, but she was still my mother. I continued to lay flowers at her grave whenever I went foraging.

A week after she fell asleep and never woke up, I dared to venture to the village, hoping that I might find some discarded food. At the bakery, I discovered some moldy bread and devoured it. Mother often went to the village to buy bread, but she rarely shared.

A woman saw me and screamed, frightening me so much that I screamed back and fled into the woods.

Abomination.

Devil child.

Monster.

I didn't dare go back. No matter how much my stomach grumbled, I sated my hunger on whatever I could forage or catch. But then, one day, I heard crying. A child of about ten sobbed in a clearing, and I had no idea what to say or do. I would almost certainly frighten her. Sticking to the shadows, I said, "Little one, why do you cry?"

The child picked up her head in alarm. "Who's there?"

"I won't hurt you," I said. "I want to help…if I can." I had never helped anyone before. Mother always said I was too infernal to do any good, even when I foraged and fed her soup when she was ill and built fires to keep her warm. But it didn't actually save her, I suppose. All my attempts at being good ended in failure.

The child scrunched her nose. "That's exactly what a monster who wants to hurt me would say."

I couldn't help but chuckle at that. When was the last time I laughed? I couldn't remember. "Fair point. But you don't seem to be in a position to turn me down."

She sighed and pulled her knees in towards her chest. "If you're gonna eat me, just eat me. It's better than waiting to die."

"You're not just lost?" I asked.

She shook her head. "I'm blind. Mostly, anyway. Can barely see two feet in front of me. The other kids decided to feed me to the monster that Goody Agnes saw. I'm of no use to the village, and so they dragged me out here as a sacrifice." She sniffled. "Mama and Papa will miss me, though. I think. Or maybe I won't be a burden to them any longer."

I descended from the tree and approached carefully. This was the closest I'd been to a human other than Mother in a very long time. "I have very little. A shack. A hearth. Some food preserves. If you don't mind my company, you are welcome to say with me."

"You won't eat me?" she asked.

"Of course not. You're too scrawny for that," I teased, and then regretted it when I saw her flinch. "Sorry. That was a joke."

"Oh," she said shakily.

"Can I take your hand?" I asked.

She nodded, and I helped her to her feet before leading her back to my lonely little shack. I had the supplies for a squirrel stew, so I quickly added it to the pot along with some herbs I'd gathered and placed it over the fire. "It shouldn't be long," I said.

She sat on the ground and curled in on herself. Though I wouldn't dare use one for myself, I took one of Mother's old blankets and wrapped it around the girl's shoulders. She pulled it tighter. "You're not just fattening me up?"

I snorted and stirred the simmering pot. "Believe me, if I wanted to fatten you up, I wouldn't be feeding you this. What can I call you?"

"I shouldn't give you my name," she said. "You might be one of the fair folk."

Huh. Perhaps that is my true parentage. I wouldn't be surprised if Mother conflated the two. "That's why I asked what I can call you, not your name," I retorted. "My mother named me Lamashtu, if that makes you feel better. But you can call me Lam, if you like." I'd always wanted to have someone call me by a nickname. Mother was never one for terms of endearment.

"After the demon? That doesn't inspire confidence." There was no heat to her words. Instead, she sounded almost amused. "I suppose you can call me Lucy."

"After the patron saint of the blind," I replied, adding a few more herbs to the pot.

"How did you know?"

"My mother made a point of teaching me about all the wonderful things I will not be a part of because of my heritage. That includes saints and a relationship with God." The stew looked about ready, so I poured her a bowl, gave her mother's old spoon, and guided her hand to where I had set the stew in front of her. Then, I poured myself one.

She wrinkled her nose. "Your mother sounds like a nightmare." Taking a spoonful of the stew, she hummed appreciatively. "I think you were lying about not fattening me up, because this is delicious."

My face heated at the compliment, and I almost wanted to cry. Mother always said my food was barely fit for the pigs. "Thank you."

"For a big, terrifying monster, you aren't so bad."

I took a spoonful of my own soup. "You just can't see me. If you did, you'd run away screaming like Goody Agnes."

She set down her spoon. "My mother likes to say that my blindness opens me to truths that others refuse to see. I can't see your monstrous exterior, but I do see your heart. I see the way you took me in, shared your food, and treated me kindly even though I'm a total stranger. That is not the heart of a monster."

This time, I did cry. Silently. Always silently. Afraid that Mother would hear and give me something to really cry about.

"Lamashtu?" Lucy's tone was anxious. Though she was a child, she carried herself like someone beyond her years. This soft, nervous voice reminded me just how young she was. "Lam? Did I say something to upset you?"

"No," I croaked. "You've said nothing wrong."

She reached out, feeling for my hand. I took it, and she gave a gentle squeeze. "And you're not a monster."

We both heard it at the same time. People calling in the woods. Calling for her. They wanted her back, and a part of me—the selfish, monstrous part of me—wanted to keep her. Instead, I said in the closest thing I had to a calm, level voice, "You should go. They're looking for you."

She surged forwards, wrapping her arms around my neck in a tight hug. "Thank you," she said.

I hugged her back, far too aware of my strength and her fragile body. All it would take is one tight squeeze and I would break her back. She was far too delicate. Too easily broken for me to love. Getting to my feet, I carried her to the door and set her down in front. "Can you find your way to your people?" I asked.

She nodded. "And I will come back once I know the way. I promise."

I wanted to tell her not to make promises she wouldn't keep. It was better to leave me alone than leave me with hope that I would see her again. That I would know genuine affection. Instead, I just said, "You are welcome whenever you want."

She wrapped her arms around my waist before dashing off into the woods, yelling, "I'm here!" at the top of her lungs.

"Lucy!" a woman cried as I shut the door. "I was so worried."

The days after I met the child were much emptier. I had gotten a taste of kindness, and now it was like a drug. I hungered for it more than food or drink, but I didn't dare find her again. She was where she belonged, so I just carried the warmth of that night close to my heart like the last stubborn ember glowing in a hearth.

A week later, I heard a knock at my door and smelled fresh bread. Opening it, I found Lucy standing on the other side with a basket of rolls and fruit and vegetable preserves. "I'm sorry it took me so long to get away," she said, "but I brought you this." She held the basket out in front of her as an offering.

Grateful, I received the gift and let her inside, listening as she chattered about the beatings the village boys got for trying to sacrifice her to a monster. Apparently, they couldn't sit down the next day. Her parents, who had always been protective of their only daughter, had been hovering like mad for the past several days, as though she might get lost in the woods again the moment that they turned their backs. She sounded vaguely annoyed, but a part of me ached. Was this what parents were supposed to do? If I had disappeared in the woods, Mother would have said, "Good riddance."

I handed her a crust of bread and a bowl of soup before pouring my own. "It's vegetable soup today." I dipped her gift in the soup and savored the taste. "This bread is delicious."

"I made it," she said, ducking her head. "I'm not much good at weaving or embroidery, but bread is easy. I help where I can."

"I'm sure it's much appreciated," I replied, tearing off another piece.

"Suppose I'm not good for much else," she muttered, taking another spoonful of soup and slurping it into her mouth.

"Nonsense," I replied. "You're good company, for one. You successfully tamed the Beast of the Wildwood."

She snorted. "I've handled kittens fiercer than you."

"Lucy, the great beast tamer," I replied and marveled at the ease of our conversation. Was this what it was like to have a friend? I hoped so. With all my heart, I hoped she would be my friend.

And for once in my life, my wish was granted. Lucy would visit every few days, always bringing fresh bread and gossip from the village. I eagerly welcomed her, like a man dying of thirst in a desert oasis. Once, she arrived with a little black bundle along with her treats. It was a kitten so small that I could hold him in the palm of one claw.

"Mama was gonna get rid of him. Says black cats are bad luck, so I stole him away with my treat basket," Lucy explained, cradling the creature to her chest, with tears budding in her eyes. "Will you take him?"

I held my hand out to her, delicately taking the little mass of black fur and bringing him to meet my eyes. His green eyes slowly closed, and a strange rumbling came from his body. I quickly handed him back to her. "I think I broke him," I said.

She giggled and stroked the top of his head. "He's purring. That means he's happy. He knows a good owner when he sees one."

I stroked him gently, painfully aware of my massive hands and his small, breakable body. He headbutted me, purring even louder. "Thank you," I whispered, holding him close as he climbed his way up my shoulders and curled between a wing and the crook of my neck. I winced at the little claws digging in like thorns. "I shall call you Bramble."

Seeming to approve, he headbutted me and licked my cheek. Lucy had a wide grin on her face as she reached up on her tiptoes and felt for him, stroking his soft fur.

And for a time, I was happy. Bramble kept me company while Lucy was away, and he proved himself to be an accomplished mouser. I had made a peaceful life for myself, alone in the woods. I never imagined a life after Mother, never thought I could feel so content.

Until Lucy burst in late one evening. She had visited that morning, so I expected that she wouldn't be around again for the next few days. I had been playing with Bramble, waving a stick around for him to chase, and we both leapt almost a foot in the air when the door slammed open. "They know about you," she said breathlessly. "I was followed. I'm so sorry Lam, I didn't know. I swear I didn't know——"

"Hey, slow down," I said, guiding her to Mother's old chair. "What happened?"

She sniffled, wiping some snot that dribbled out her nose. "Some boys followed me into the woods. W-when they saw you, they told the adults in the village, and now they're calling me a witch, and they're coming to kill you, and maybe me too. I'm sorry. I'm so sorry. Please forgive me."

I wiped the tears from her face. "It's okay. It's not your fault."

"There it is," someone shouted from the outside.

She clutched me, her little body shivering in terror as she mumbled her apologies into my shoulder.

"Demon! I know you're in there!" a man shouted. "Free the girl you've bewitched, or we will show no mercy!"

An idea struck me then. A painful one, but necessary. Some weeks ago, I had made a straw basket so that I could carry Bramble while I flew. I got to my feet and shoved a few meager necessities into it before setting a protesting Bramble inside and shutting it. Even with the extra weight, the basket still fit well enough between my wings.

"What are you doing?" Lucy asked quietly.

I knelt in front of her and wiped away her tears. My heart felt as though it would shatter, but I knew this was the right thing to do for all of us. When Mother fell asleep and never woke, I felt no sense of grief, only guilt for being so okay with her death. With Lucy, though, it felt like I was ripping out a piece of my own heart "I need you to trust me and do exactly as I say. If they want a monster, I'll give them a monster. And after tonight, that's all I am to you—a monster."

"Come out before we burn you out!" another villager shouted from the outside.

"You're not, though. You're good."

I pulled her into another hug. "Thank you for seeing the good in me. Now, though, you have to pretend." I scooped her up. "Play dead and go limp in my arms. I promise everything will be okay."

A window shattered, and the dry kindling inside my shack erupted into flame. Bramble yowled in terror. With a roar, I kicked the door open, Lucy limp in my arms. "Curses! I thought my plan of pretending to be a kindly old woman to trick the blind girl would work, but you mortals are too strong for—"

"Open fire!" one of the men shouted.

And then a chorus of "Kill the demon!" and "Kill the witch!" followed, drowning out Lucy's parents' cries of protest. They shot wildly, their bullets striking the burning shack behind me. Lucy gasped, then went limp. With a cry, I flew upwards, desperate to keep my precious cargo safe. Bullets ripped holes in my wings, the iron burning like the flames that once filled my hearth. I landed near the entrance of a nearby cave and staggered to a halt. Bramble cried out as I hastily set Lucy's body down. Crimson bloomed from a bullet hole in her side.

Lucy stared up sightlessly, choking on the blood that trickled from her lips.

"Lucy," I said, stroking her cheek. "Lucy, can you hear me?"

"Lam?" came the response, barely weaker than a whisper. "Lam, something's wrong. I'm scared."

"You're all right. You're going to be all right." I clutched her close, which caused her to weakly cry out. "Lucy, please don't die. Please. You're my only friend."

No matter how I begged, pleaded, or in my desperation, called out for the intervention of my demonic father, she still took in a shuttering breath and breathed out her last. And my grief became a rage unlike anything I'd ever known. The rage burrowed into my heart like maggots into a corpse. For once in my life, I had been happy. I thought, perhaps, that I was more than an abomination. More than a devil child. More than a monster. I was something worthy of love. And they ripped it all away from me. They killed her like she was nothing. Like she didn't matter. The innocent blind girl who was so kind that she showed a monster what it meant to love.

Bramble headbutted me, demanding attention. Heart soothing a little, I scooped him up and placed a kiss on the top of his head. "Stay with her, love. I'll be back."

Despite my wounds, despite the tears nearly blinding me, despite the weight of my grief threatening to crush me, I flew. The villagers, guided by torchlight, searched the woods for us. Looking to finish the job. I landed quietly behind one of the village men. He barely had time to speak before I tore his head from his shoulders, unleashing a fountain of blood.

I spotted another and flew into him, straddling his body and ripping out his still-beating heart.

"There it is!" a woman shouted, and the sound of gunshots filled the forest. But this only inspired more rage. With a guttural howl, I charged the woman and snatched her rifle. I broke it in two and stabbed her with the pointed shards before retreating to the treetops.

"We'll have its head on a pike!"

"They'll tell stories of us! We'll be saints!"

"I know these woods! It can't have gone far!"

They thought they knew the woods, but I was a creature born of the woods, raised there. I was as much a part of the forest as it was a part of me, and I was ready to show these vile creatures what a true monster looks like.

I picked them off one by one, ripping them apart with my teeth and claws, gutting them until my hair was sticky and matted with blood. Only two villagers remained. They knelt before my burning shack and sobbed. One of them was a woman that could have been Lucy in twenty years—her mother.

They didn't notice me when I flew off, and barely noticed when I returned, Bramble secured in his basket and Lucy in my arms. I laid their daughter in front of them, and her mother sobbed, holding her close.

Her father drew his pistol. "Get away from us, you monster."

"I would never have harmed your daughter," I said. "She was a kind soul and a good friend. My only friend. I hope she finds peace."

His finger hovered over the trigger. "Liar."

Removing Bramble's basket, I closed my eyes, preparing for the crack of thunder and burning pain. *I'm sorry, Bramble. Hopefully, you'll be okay without me.*

"Wait." Lucy's mother got to her feet, her daughter's blood staining her dress. She placed her hand on top of her husband's pistol and lowered it. "Leave it. There's been enough death tonight."

Not taking his eyes off me, he holstered his pistol and scooped up Lucy's body. Without another word, the small family walked away, leaving me and Bramble alone in the ashes of the only home I've ever known.

I picked up his basket and carried him deeper into the woods and farther away from a world that hates us.

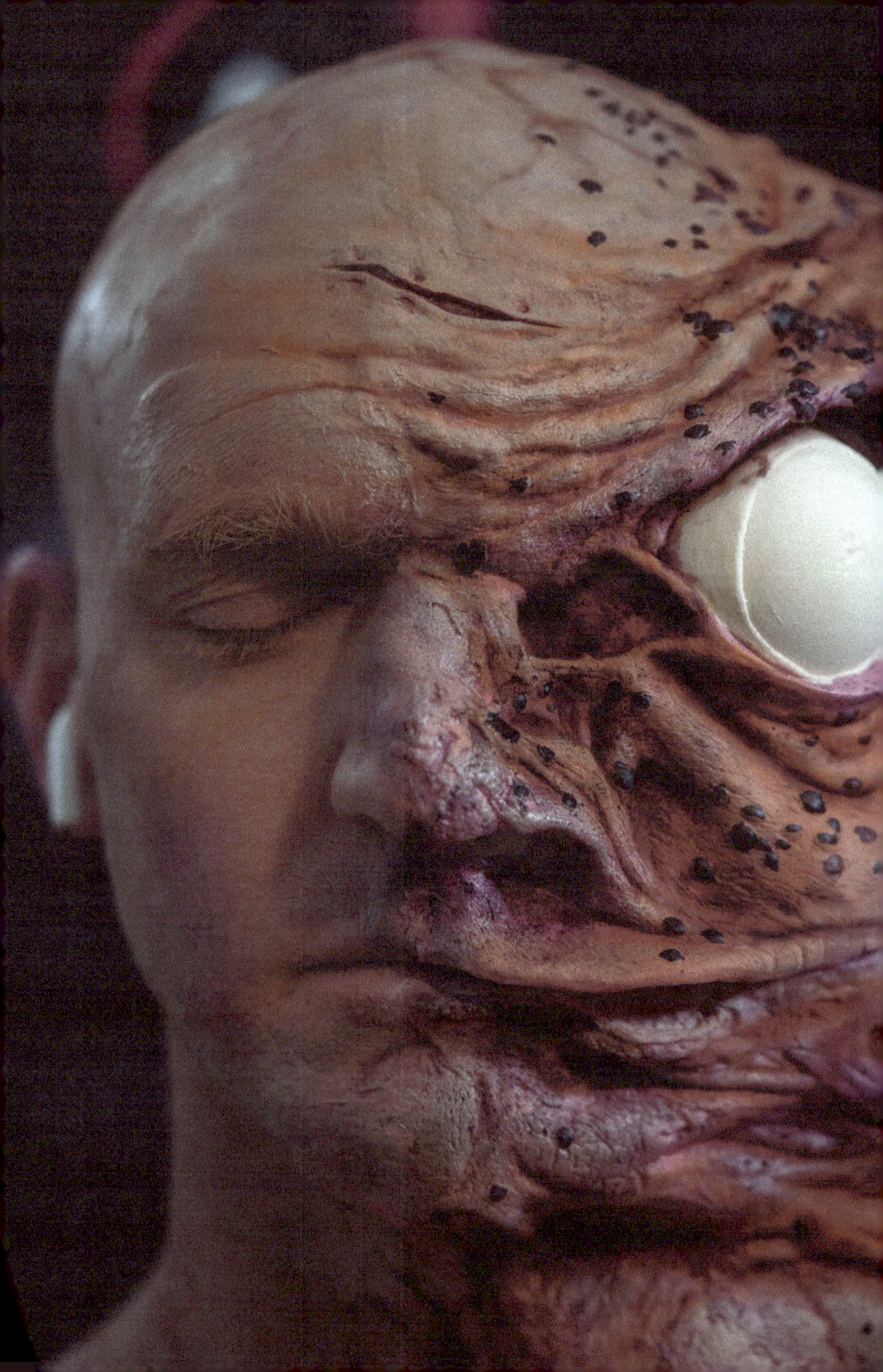

TOAD BOYS

Art by Dennis Preston
Feature by Phil McLaughlin

Dennis Preston is a special effects makeup artist, filmmaker, and illustrator, with a fondness for horror and gore. Through his company, Preston Perspectives, he creates special effects for films and music videos, which include a number of sculptures and prosthetics that are worthy of your worst nightmares. It's a tedious job driven by curiosity, experimentation, risk-taking, and the willingness to get a little bloody in the process.

I met Dennis a couple of years ago while in the early planning stages for my own short horror film, *Toad Boy,* which is screening at genre festivals this fall. The artistry and enthusiasm he brought to the project was instrumental in our early success and led to acceptances by Toronto After Dark, Telluride Horror Show, and Knoxville Horror Film Fest, to name a few. He was even nominated for Best Makeup Effects from HorrorFest International in St. George, Utah.

It was an honor to collaborate with Dennis and a blast to catch up with him for this interview.

PHIL MCLAUGHLIN: Were you always drawn to horror films? What are some of your favorite movies?

Pictured left: *Toad Boy makeup nearly complete after airbrush and detail work (Photo by Hoss Fatemi)*

DENNIS PRESTON: I honestly didn't start watching horror films until later in high school. I always thought horror films were just dumb and not my thing. This, of course, was because I had never actually watched a horror film. A lot of them are dumb (which I think is part of their charm), but many are brilliant and can inspire some unique conversations. I truly believe that the horror genre has the largest and most loyal and loving fan base. You just don't get the same kind of community with comedy or action. As for my favorites: *Aliens, The Descent, Chucky, The Feast,* and *Rubber.*

PM: When did you know you wanted to pursue a career in practical and special effects? What sort of training or schooling did you pursue?

Pictured above: *Toad Boy sculpture (Photo by Dennis Preston)*

DP: I attended the American Academy of Art in Chicago, where I got a BFA in Illustration. While at school, I came across a promotional flyer on the community board from J. Anthony Kosar, an alumni who was teaching mask-making classes. I took the half-mask course, full-head mask-making, airbrush, and then the makeup effects class where I learned how to sculpt, mold, mix, pour, and apply my own foam latex prosthetics. It was during this time that I worked on my first film as a special effects makeup artist. The film was never released, but after that experience, I knew I wanted to do this for the rest of my life.

PM: Are there specific artists, films, or television shows that directly influenced or challenged you?

Pictured top: *Toad Boy camera-ready (Photo by Hoss Fatemi)*

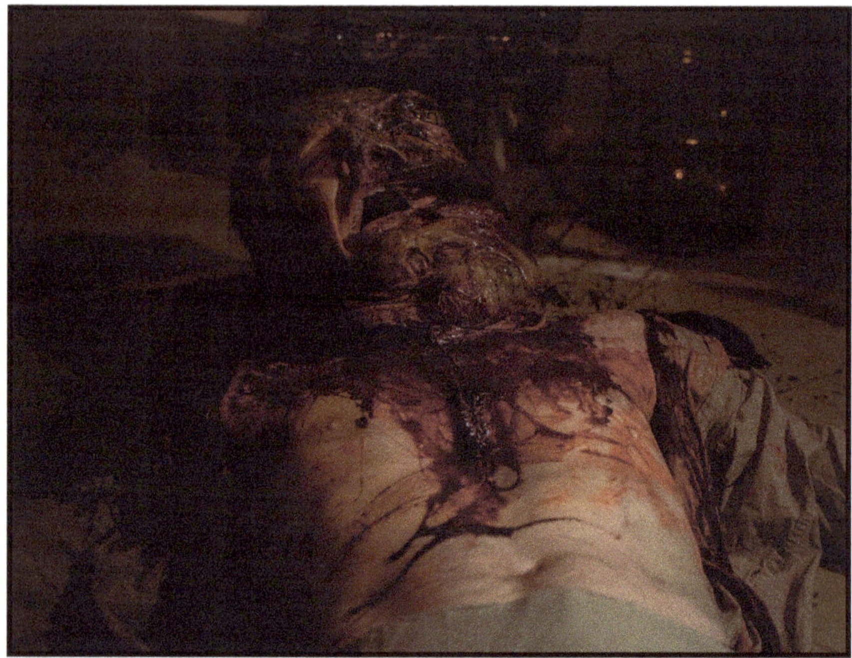

DP: Character designer and sculptor, Jordu Schell, has definitely influenced me in how I go about my sculptures. But I don't think there are any specific films or TV shows that directly influence me. Anything that has a cool makeup or practical effect makes me excited to try it for myself—and make it look realistic.

PM: What's the most challenging build or effect you've done? The most fun?

DP: Every project presents new challenges that I welcome with open arms, but I would say that *Toad Boy* was my most extensive and challenging make-up to date. It was the first time I needed to break up a sculpture into pieces and float it off the initial lifecast. This means after working for hours upon hours on the creature sculpture and perfecting it, I had to take a knife to it and cut it up (strategically, of course). The fun part was actually figuring out the best places to cut the sculpture so that during application with the actor, I could create a seamless edge as if it was still one complete piece. It was a lot of fun! That's the best part about projects—not only designing a creature or character but figuring out the best wake to make it a reality. Although very tedious at times, I truly enjoy it!

Pictured top: *Actor Cliff Chamberlain after eight hours in Toad Boy makeup (Photo by Hoss Fatemi)*

PM: How has your process evolved over time? Are there resources you turn to when taking on a new project?

DP: My time management and efficiency have improved immensely. As with anything you do over time, you get better at it.

As for resources, I'm lucky to have a great network of friends I can reach out to if I have questions about something that I am unfamiliar with or unsure of. There are also numerous books I can turn to, and the Stan Winston School has an enormous library of courses available online. I've been doing special effects for ten years now, but I'm always learning.

PM: What about *Toad Boy* drew you to the project?

DP: Honestly, I was excited to meet when I learned you were an editor on *Fear the Walking Dead* because I really enjoy the show. But as we talked more and more abut what you were hoping to achieve with *Toad Boy,* I knew I wanted to get to work and design this character. I love projects that present a challenge and allow me to explore a new process or technique.

PM: What was the process for the hero makeup effect in *Toad Boy*? From design to production - and what happens on the day?

Pictured above: *SPFX Makeup Assistant Noelle Hetzel (left), actor Cliff Chamberlain (center), Dennis Preston (right) (Photo by Hoss Fatemi)*

DP: First, we went back and forth discussing the look of Toad Boy with reference images. I then used those images to develop sketches and color studies until we were satisfied with the look.

Then, before I could move on to sculpting, we needed to make the lifecast of the actor. This is the process of taking a mold of the actor's head, neck, and shoulders so I can sculpt the prosthetic directly onto the mold. This process allows the prosthetics to fit perfectly on the actor who will be wearing them. Once I have the initial positive of the actor, I make necessary corrections, clean up imperfections, and then make a second mold so I can have a proper bust to sculpt on.

After the sculpture was complete, it was time to figure out how to cut it up into sections—making a one-piece prosthetic wasn't practical. I ended up cutting the sculpture into four pieces and then floated the sculpture.

We now move onto a second bust of the actor (this bust is able to be put into the oven). I use the four floated pieces and apply them to the stone bust before making "snaps." Snaps are individual molds made of the pieces or sections of the sculpture that were cut in the previous steps. Once the molds are made, they are filled with foam latex and sit in the oven for hours.

Pictured top: *Sculptures on display at Dennis Preston's workshop*

Now we bring our four foam latex pieces to set. We applied a bald cap to the actor, Cliff Chamberlain, to keep his hair clean and then, like a puzzle, we added each of the four pieces to the actor. The edges were blended, then painting started with a base coat before airbrushing. The toad eye was hand-painted and finished with a coat of clear epoxy to make it look glossy. Add a wig piece, and we had ourselves a monster.

The process on set took almost 8.5 hours. I'd like to add, Cliff Chamberlain was phenomenal, sitting as still as a statue for those eight hours. One of the best I've ever had in my chair.

PM: You also constructed our reptilian homage to the *Necronomicon*, the *Necromagica*, as well as helped with some dead body makeup and scarring effects. Is the process any different with these?

DP: It's definitely a lot less intensive. More out of the kit than requiring any in-shop prep.

PM: Still, the level of detail is evident, even in these less intense effects. Thank you again for bringing your expertise to the project. Your work is a significant factor in the festival success of the film and the leading subject of praise from festival programmers and fellow filmmakers.

Looking ahead, is there an effect or build you've always wanted to do?

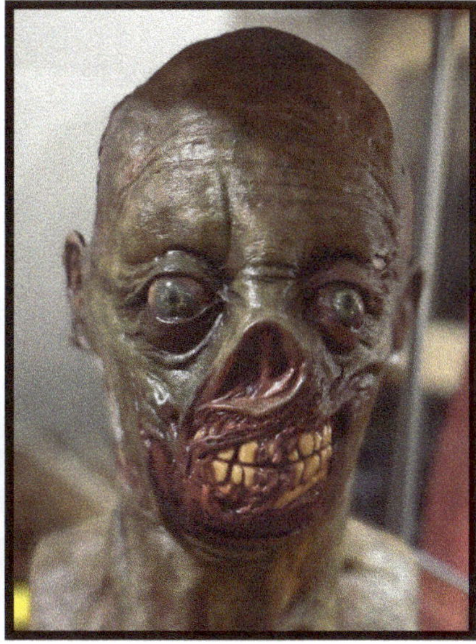

Pictured above: *More sculptures on display at Dennis Preston's workshop*

DP: I really want the opportunity to create something large, like *Jurassic Park* T-Rex large. Or maybe *Lake Placid* crocodile large. Something that requires an entire team of artists to bring to life!

PM: Last question: store bought blood or homemade?

DP: I prefer to make my own blood.

For more information, pictures, and links to Dennis Preston's social media, please visit prestonperspectives.com.

For information on Toad Boy, including a trailer and upcoming festival screenings, please visit toadboyfilm.com.

Pictured top row: *Two stages of sculpting (Photos by Dennis Preston)* **Bottom:** *Actor Cliff Chamberlain (left) and Director Phil McLaughlin (right) (Photo by Hoss Fatemi)*

TOAD BOY
FREAK
OFFICIAL SELECTION
TORONTO AFTER DARK FILM FESTIVAL
OFFICIAL SELECTION
HORROR SHOW
FILMQUEST
OFFICIAL SELECTION
NIGHTMARES FILM FESTIVAL 2023
OFFICIAL SELECTION
KNOXVILLE HORROR FILM FEST 2023
TOHORROR Fantastic Film Fest
OFFICIAL SELECTION 2023
ABERTOIR HORROR FESTIVAL
OFFICIAL SELECTION
WALES 2023
OFFICIAL SELECTION
HORROR HAUS 2023
OFFICIAL SELECTION
HORROR FEST INTERNATIONAL 2023
NOMINEE BEST MAKEUP EFFECTS
HORROR FEST INTERNATIONAL 2023
2023 OFFICIAL SELECTION
CHICAGO HORROR FILM FESTIVAL
NOMINEE 2023
CHICAGO HORROR FILM FESTIVAL
A NIGHT OF HORROR INTERNATIONAL FILM FESTIVAL
OFFICIAL SELECTION 2023
OFFICIAL SELECTION
SOHO HORROR FILM FESTIVAL 2023
ids can be so cruel.

HOTEL LEVIATHAN

THE DICHOTOMY OF A BEAST

by Eygló Karlsdóttir

I wished for you.

The soft blue flowers always sway delicately back and forth in your hair. I placed them there myself as a reminder, and you didn't seem to mind, not then and not now. You just smile at me, quiet in my presence as if you are making sure I am as much me as I possibly can be, with the beast up close and personal.

The sound from the others is like the chattering of birds, millions of birds. It etches itself into one's soul with each individual voice growing a seed of their own, and I quickly long for silence, thinking of the way I can shout your name and how the silence afterwards always feels more tangible, without a stain or strain. We're in tethers, and I often do shout your name over the ocean of people. You stand so still, like a ghost in the crowd, except somehow you seem clearer than all the others. Tangible, while the others aren't.

Time confuses me.

And you can't hear me. You have your back turned, and you are probably talking to someone more interesting. I turn away, wondering why the vision of the flower in your hair seems so sad, almost hostile. The hotel is my home, but I'll never get used to it. Never feel as if I belong. I never feel safe.

The elevator is particular. You have to push the fourth-floor button extra hard and hold it in for a little while before it will take. When it does, the thing seems to shift slightly, and then the elevator starts to crawl upwards.

At the fourth floor, I exit the elevator and head to my room. The beast we call The Leviathan is sleeping softly. I can hear the trickle, the sick murky sound of it shifting slightly before it settles again. I lie down on my bed. The gulls are flying outside the window, but they, too, are silent. A slumber comes over me, and I fall asleep with your silhouette burned on my retinas.

It seems to belong there.

When I wake up, I feel a strong urge to urinate. The darkness is thick, but I find my way to the bathroom, open the door, and sit down, relieved to let go. When I'm finished, I get up, flush, and wash my hands. I've almost made it to the bed again when it starts.

The rumbling. The noise. The loud roar of the beast.

I cover my ears.

"Good lord, I've awoken it," I find myself muttering. I wonder if I'll find you if I leave my room to search, but I know it's hopeless because it's late, and you're fast asleep somewhere in the hotel, and I don't know where.

Even if I did know where you are, I wouldn't want to wake you, because that's not how this works. Instead, I make sure the bed covers are tucked tightly around the mattress, and then I slip beneath them and hide.

The noise is unbearable while it lasts, but then the beast groans one final time, and it's quiet again. Dormant, but on its guard. It's always on guard. Always has been. Always will be. It's watching me. Keeping track of us.

The Leviathan. The monstrosity. The unknown eldritch abomination.

When the first rays of the sun start to show themselves, I get dressed quickly and go outside. It's the best part of the day, the time when I can freely roam about town, walk down the slope to the beach and follow it until I can climb up the hill towards the castle.

I've seen many things on the hill. Spooks both alive and dead, doing questionable things. They linger in the shadows in the early morning, and I can pass by and pretend I don't see them. Just like I pretended not to see you that morning when the seagulls raged in the sky, chasing a bird away that wasn't one of their own. You were looking at the view, the sea, and at the Ferris wheel, and I wondered what you were thinking, what you feared, what you longed for, and I wondered, even then, what it would be like to be a part of your life, have a place in that soul of yours that glows, still to this day, fiercer than any soul I've ever seen before.

It wasn't until later that you saw me. It wasn't until later that I realized you *could* see me. The whiteness of my hair, the redness of my eyes, the grayness of my skin, and you didn't fear me, not like the others. Instead, you reached out to touch me, and when your finger brushing away a strand of hair that had fallen into my eye, I felt it starting.

I felt everything change.

You reached forward and touched me that day, fearless, pitiless, as if you found me interesting, not hideous, and maybe even slightly human. You didn't look at my sharp teeth, my shifty, shapeless nature. Instead, you saw the softness of my skin and the brightness in my eyes.

You, with the tousled black hair and dark, prying eyes. I felt the soft rhythm of your heart and the gentle hesitation in your body language, as if you were bursting to ask me who I was and where I'd been all your life but didn't know how to force the words from your mouth.

And I don't know how to tell you what you did for me then, when the murky hardened bit of my soul softened, became tar, and started, ever so slowly, to dissolve, its dark remains oozing into the walls, going into the floors, the carpet, the chairs, and everything else around me.

The castle isn't free from The Leviathan. Neither is the hotel, and I wonder as I pass the castle how many buildings in town are infested with it, this dark beast that's gigantic but can also penetrate the smallest spaces, like the inner corners of your soul—*my* soul.

I start zigzagging through the streets, slowly finding my way back, content to linger in the early hours when no one else is around. I look through the windows and contemplate the decorations they leave in their yards, the dissolving houses and the light that changes once the sun is high.

Back at the hotel, a few people are prowling the premises, quietly invading. They find their spots and do their best to ignore the world around them while their brains reacclimate to the eternity of hollowness the hotel forces upon its guests. I hear someone complain about the gulls. Another one agrees, but then the silence is broken by a squawk from outside.

It makes me laugh.

I usually know my place during the day, hiding in my room on the fourth floor, biding my time, but whenever the guests start to make too much noise, I leave my room and head down to the lounge, or to the bar, or even into the old ballroom, where I sometimes sneak a peek into the cellar and descend quietly into the cave-like underground. I roam the subterranean maze and try not to remember the many disturbing parties that played out down there in that hideaway—the vile behavior, the orgies, the cult rituals that seemed never to end. They let The Leviathan in, called for it, yearned for it, longed to merge with it, and now…

I shouldn't be here. I can see through the walls and into its innards. I can see the destruction, the depravity, the defecation.

I venture into the lounge and sit down one of the soft sofas, let the sun warm my hands as I look out the old windows at the sea, at the horizon, at the "not-here." I watch the sun arc slowly across the sky until the chatter in the room suddenly gets louder. The empty room is now filled with dinner guests, all holding glasses of alcohol and leaning forward to hear one another above the din. The faces around me beam, thrilled by the excitement in the room, but I just feel exhausted. I'm rattled by the way these people sneak up on me, and I find myself wanting to melt into the floor. I want to become one with the furniture, never be seen again.

I want to vanish.

Which is an odd thing to want, I guess, considering that I'm already invisible to them. They might feel an immediate sense of displeasure when near me, but they can't actually see me. No one can, except you.

I'm reminded of the night we first met, and how you looked at me from across this same room, a shy smile on your face. Our eyes met, and I could tell it was me you were looking at and not someone else. It was not just a case of you looking through me at the person standing behind me. There was only the window behind me, the view, and the sea. You walked across the floor to me, stopping only once to acknowledge someone who wanted to greet you. It was someone you knew and for a sad second, I feared you were going to get stuck there, that you would never get away, and that we would be standing at different ends of the room forever, never to actually meet.

But then you bowed your head to the person, and you continued your way across the room toward me. A bubbling, tar-like substance appeared beneath your footsteps then, tried to grab a hold of you, tried to stop you, but your stride was perfectly timed, perfectly executed, the perfect speed.

And then you were here.

You *are* here. Looking me in the eyes in a way I haven't been looked at for what feels like centuries. I saw, and I see, the tar vanish from the floor, and though I know it'll be back, because it just needs to gather its strength, I find I don't care. It can devour me whole, finally, after all this time. It will be worth it for this moment of staring into your eyes, listening to your voice as you start talking to me as if we already know each other.

And we do. Because of course we do. Because we have done this all before. We stood here before and stared into each other's eyes.

I pull the Forget-Me-Nots from my dress and place them gently in your hair. The others can smell the flowers, but they can't see them.

These charms have protected me for so long, this never-ending beauty that blossoms into exploding blue stars. They've protected me from this place, from The Leviathan and from the darkness that has threatened to overtake me. But now they're yours, all yours, and I wouldn't have it any other way.

I feel myself fading away, but you grab my hand.

"Where are you going?" you ask, and I cock my head at you.

"Nowhere," I tell you. "There's nowhere else I'd rather be." I whisper the words, half hoping you'll hear me, fearing you won't. I see the tar appearing in the corners of the room, the blackness spreading across the tapestries and along the painted walls. It'll soon get us, but you'll be safe because I've kept you safe. Because of the flowers.

"Will you go somewhere quiet with me?" you ask, and I nod.

You take my hand and together we traipse out of the room as if there is no tomorrow. As if we haven't already played out this part of our journey a thousand times before. It's as if you, too, see the darkness spreading, see The Leviathan's immense anger manifest in response to someone seeing me, to *you* seeing me, seeing my faded figure. You pull me along the corridor and down the red-carpeted stairs that smell of urine and something else I've never been able to identify. Then we push open the doors and we're in the cave cellar.

It's the most dangerous place in the building. Why are you pulling me in here? But the thought vanishes as I feel your light and your hands touching my skin. You push me to the wall by the door and gently put your lips on mine. It's the most intimate sensation, and it takes my breath away, steals it from my lungs, and all I can do is answer your thirst, your hunger, with my own. I remember the flowers and that you are protected, even down here you are protected, and so I pull you closer, wanting you, wanting your body pressed against mine. Sturdy, hungry, and…

…The tremble isn't just from the hunger I feel for you. It's something else, the memory of this place plaguing my bones, the old, infested grounds seeping into my soul, overtaking what's left of me. I remember the rituals, the sacrifices we made. This beast will get into you as well, will get you if I let it. I try to pull away, but it's too tempting to keep you close just a little longer, and soon I'm pulling at your clothes, pulling at your pants, the thrill of your touch doing things to me I didn't know were possible. The white in my hair washes away to reveal a youthful brown beneath. I can see it in the strands of hair falling into my eyes. You kiss them shut, and then primal instinct takes over. The Leviathan may be controlling us, but I don't care. I want more. More of you. More of your touch.

Afterwards, when I'm lying in your arms on the floor, I see the black tar everywhere. I lean forward and kiss you again. This time there is less hunger. Gentleness. And I see The Leviathan's footprints recede somewhat.

"It'll get us eventually," I whisper. "You have to get away from this place. You can still leave."

"I don't want to leave," you whisper, softly stroking my hair. The white turns brown again beneath your fingers. It is as if your touch colors my skin, colors my hair, colors all the things I wear. And I know you see the fear in my eyes because you smile.

"You're here still, aren't you?"

I touch your cheek, place the palm of my hand softly on your skin and stroke you. "Why would you stay when there's a world out there? A world of beautiful creatures, more beautiful than myself? Places safer than this one? Why would you stay?"

You don't say anything, just kiss me again and shake your head as if I'm the one who doesn't understand. The sound of footsteps alerts us, but neither of us moves from the spot on the floor.

"Is it a spook or a troop?" you ask, and I listen more carefully.

"Not a spook," I whisper back. "They don't make sounds like these."

"But you do," you tell me, and I feel the tar quickly retreating, as if it's scurrying away from something very unpleasant.

"I'm so happy that I found you," you tell me.

"I'm so happy you found me. And I'm sorry you're going to be stuck here because of it."

"I'm not," you say.

In my room on the fourth floor, we sometimes sleep like the dead. The sound of The Leviathan still stirs in the walls and in the floors—loud, angry, agitated—but the noise is not as disturbing as it used to be. When I awaken, there is a gull outside the windowsill, pecking at the glass. A tap, tap, tapping sound emanates from the window, but you sleep through it, tired from last night's ordeal, tired from wading through all the corruption and filth inside the cave.

I watch you sleep for a while and wonder to myself how long it will take before you resent me for being stuck here, unable to leave. Because The Leviathan will never let us leave, not now.

You pull the Forget-Me-Nots from of your hair and hand me one but keep the other. The flowers won't grant us the power to leave, but they're strong enough to keep the darkness away, maybe forever.

The Leviathan screams, shakes in its hiding place so the entire floor rumbles. You stir slightly in your sleep but continue breathing peacefully. You sleep so beautifully.

One day, the monster will become more awake than ever before, and when it finally awakens completely and devours the entire shore, leaves nothing but the seagulls in the sky, at least I will know I had been seen.

And when that time comes, I will pull the Forget-Me-Not from my hair, the beautiful flower that's been keeping me safe, the twin flowers that are supposed to be keeping us both safe, and I'll place mine behind your ear, and I will wish you away, just as I wished you with all my heart into being.

You, who saw all my flaws and loved me anyway. You, who defy my darkness with a smile that would light up the sun. You, who were made by The Leviathan and can be undone by The Leviathan.

By me.

I stir, jealous in my slumber. I will never let you go.

RETSNOM

by Rowan Hill

His grandaddy's Civil War saber was a rusty and curved thing that swung on Leon's hip like a second dick needing caressing. So that's exactly what a cocksure hunter like Leon did—caressed it with his fingertips. Trudging through the Louisiana bayou, he smirked, happy to be outfitted with such a fine weapon and his fine three-piece suit while questing for his next big score. Gold locks stuck sweaty to his forehead, and the collar of his white shirt had turned yellow in the humidity, but he didn't mind being overdressed so long as he cut a dashing figure.

His pale blue eyes climbed the bald cypress trees, towering overhead like goliaths, Spanish moss swaying from the branches like gray drapes in a breeze. He then looked down to the slithering tail tracks in the mud, evidence a large gator called this riverbank home.

"Where did he say this place was?" Leon asked the man trailing steps behind.

His partner on the expedition, Ray, squinted and rubbed his temples. A blue haint had infected Ray's eyesight a few days back, and it was causing him the worst of headaches. He wondered if this was the start of color blindness or something more serious. He removed his bifocals and wiped the thick condensation from the lenses. Ray pointed east. "That way. Beyond the boulder with the Injun pictures on it. Not much farther."

Leon gripped the saber confidently. "Right then. Let's go slay us a big ole' monster, huh?" he said gleefully, stomping on the bracken, loud enough to warn any snakes nearby. Ray followed.

"You really gonna use that thing on a monster?"

Leon smirked. "You jealous?"

"Naw, it's a bit ostentatious, is all. We don't get paid extra for style. Gun seems smarter."

Leon stopped, the smirk leaving his face for something more sinister. "Heard you called on my Marie last week."

Ray's throat hitched like it was dry, maybe even sore with the start of a cold, and he ran a clammy hand through his short black hair. "C'mon, Leon. Marie and I are just old school friends. You know that."

"Uh-huh." Leon fingered the sword's brass handle. "A twenty-year-old woman looking like Marie with a fiancé don't have male *friends*, Ray. You trying to cuckold me?" He stopped and turned his broad shoulders to slim Ray, a full head taller than him.

Ray adjusted his bifocals just in time to see a muscle twitch in Leon's square jaw.

"I like you, Ray," said Leon. "I do. Always good to have a smart friend, one with a car and a fancy degree, one who can play the piano at the Governor's parties while I sing." He paused and the bayou critters also stayed silent as if waiting for him to finish his thought. But the tension in Leon's face dissolved into another smirk, and he continued walking. He spoke over his shoulder. "Tell you what? You help me bag this beast, and I'll let you take Marie out for a ride or two." He met Ray's eyes as they walked, and the smaller man looked to his feet. Leon smiled. "What's a ride or two between friends?"

After trekking a mile east, the bayou gave way to drier woodlands.

"Did we go too far?" Leon asked.

Ray searched, squinting through his foggy lenses and growing headache, and pointed to a boulder the color of sand a hundred yards in the distance. "Nope. That's exactly the rock we're looking for."

Native American petroglyphs were inscribed on the boulder. Worn by time and erosion, the muddy red symbols were too faded to be legible.

"What's it say?" Leon asked.

Ray leaned in. "Mmm, can't tell exactly, but looks like a warning."

"Sounds like we're close then."

Ray blinked the blue film from his eyes, uneasiness creeping over his scalp. His hands were empty. "I feel like I should have a weapon. One sword between the two of us doesn't seem—"

Leon drew the saber from its sheath. "I didn't bring you along for muscle, Ray." He eyed the man's slender frame with contempt. "You're here to navigate, help carry the carcass back after I kill it. Maybe help me skin it, if that's even possible."

They rounded the boulder, the hill inclining into a lip the men walked around. The ground beneath their feet immediately changed. There was no woodland detritus or fallen leaves. No bushes or tracks. A young tree had fallen at one time and was decayed almost to particles, a thick line of debris. Buds of flowers stood next to stiff stems of roses months past dead within the log's corpse. Ray noticed the white of clean bones of maybe a child scattered in the fallen tree.

Before Ray could draw attention to his grim findings, the sweetest of all sounds filled the air. An angel, a woman, crooned a tune Ray recognized from church. An old bayou gospel floating on the heavy air.

That old-time religion…

It's good enough for me….

The singing voice, soft as warm butter and smooth as velvet, grew clearer as the pair rounded the hill and faced the open mouth of a cave. The cave opening was the blackest pitch Ray had witnessed at midday, and it was taller than Leon and twice as wide. Just past the radial of sunlight, the ground inside descended quickly, the innards drawing down and in.

It's good when I'm in trouble…

And it's good enough for me…

Leon stabbed his saber into the ground and leaned on the hilt like a cane. He turned a skeptical eye to Ray, raptured by the husky voice. "What kind of woman you suppose sings gospel way out here in the middle of cursed Injun lands?"

Before Ray could reply, the woman stopped singing, an urgency in her tone as if she'd come in mid-conversation.

"*Are you men? How many are you?*" she asked. Leon's eyebrows shot up, a question forming when the woman suddenly began crying, her voice acquiring a tinny quality in the cave.

"*Is someone out there?*" she asked, calmer, and all at once, the blue film in Ray's sight crescendoed to a flash and he dug the heels of his palms into them. The woman was abruptly crying again, halfway through a great lamentation.

"*Please, help, I've been stuck here for days, maybe longer! I can't tell. Time is funny down here…*"

"What you think?" Ray murmured. Leon, confused at the unusual one-sided conversation, bunched his forehead together and opened his mouth to speak when she interrupted his next thought.

"Please be quick! It might come back. I never know when it's coming back!"

Leon pulled his sword from the ground and gripped the brass dick tight, ready for the unseen threat. "Now just slow down, darlin'. What's coming back? Something trapped you down there?"

"I have money! My daddy is rich! He owns a big plantation south of Lake Charles." Her voice ricocheted from the different corners of the cave.

Leon raised a confused eyebrow at the erratic nature of her conversation, the way it heightened and altered in pitch and breath. But the corner of his mouth curled up at the magic word, *"money."*

"Well, whatchu say, Raymond? Feel like rescuing a rich debutante instead?"

Raymond blinked the blue from his eyes, his throat throbbing sore now, and shrugged noncommittally. Leon snatched his collar, dragging him. "Come on, Brains," he muttered and crossed the clearing to the cave, stopping at the line of sunshine.

There was a moment, a fraction of a breath where the pair unanimously paused at the cave's lip like fear was a literal barrier. A precipice. Hesitation was the only sign of weakness from headstrong Leon before he pulled them both past the line of shadow, and they were inside.

An odor, the reek of decomposing flesh, twitched the insides of Ray's nose. It came from the pitch-black maw of the cave's guts, and as he reached for his handkerchief, the bright blue light flashed at the back of the cave, searing Ray's eyeballs like a blinding wave crashed on top of him, a *chittering* voice flooding his brain.

Ray's body jerked, falling like gravity yanked him, and both men lay prostrate at the bottom of the wet cave. Confused and disorientated at their sudden position, Ray flinched as Leon shrieked, his mouth now sliced open across his cheek, shredded into flesh-flaps. His attention drew down Leon's body to a shadow of pitch straddling him, melding with black air. It crouched and sank onto his chest. A line of darkness curled away from the void to expose two rows of neon-white teeth, each tooth dagger-sharp. They begin snipping the air, turning down to Leon's belly, and began plucking his viscera with the frenzied appetite of a bloodthirsty carrion eater, his three-piece ruined. Ray was paralyzed, frozen, his scream stifled when freezing hands solidified from the shadows and scrambled up his legs.

Two hands. Three. More. Bony fingers, knobby and ice-like, strong, pawing past his warm groin, up his chest, his neck, caressing the stubble on his chin.

They searched Ray's face like a blind man. One crawled onto his lips, a digging grub burrowing past and inside. The callused finger stroked his tongue.

Ray gagged, then bit down hard.

The cold fingers were more bone than flesh. More acid than blood. But Ray gritted his teeth, the fingers wiggling like caught worms. Cold, acrid blood, glowing phosphorescent blue, trickled down his throat. A frost sizzled his nerves and gullet, and the *chittering* scream echoed in his mind. The darkness eating Leon suddenly had eyes in the middle of its pitch body, two neon-blue jewels appearing above the shadow's mouth. They turned their ire to Ray. The darkness gasped and blue light engulfed Ray.

Ray blinked, his arms akimbo, unfathomably back atop of the cave's incline. *Hadn't he just been...?* He searched down the hill where he had... once been thrown? Violated? His heart raced, and his mouth tasted sour. Standing with squared shoulders, Leon chortled, his cheek un-maimed. He held the saber aloft.

"Now, darlin', this ain't funny. I wore my nicest suit and best smile to come on in here and rescue you. Where you hidin'? Don't you want us to save you?" His voice trembled. A terrible foreboding clinched Ray's sore throat when the angel spoke.

"*I'm over here, pinned to the floor.*" She was unexpectedly close. Both men spun to the cave's wall where a pair of motionless blanched feet lay, naked and dirty in the soft gloom.

Ray didn't want any closer, angel or not. He felt on the edge of remembering something terribly, life-savingly important. The back of his throat burned like he just drank glacial water. Leon reached and snatched Ray's shoulder for an anchor, and the pair approached her.

"*I need some help getting up, please...*"

In the gloam, the inert feet connected to a naked pair of slender legs, lily-white thighs leading to a naked groin and a tuft of black hair. Ray froze. Above the groin, a deep crevice gouged her belly. Simply blackness, the start of a black hole.

Leon murmured, "What in damnation..." He inched closer, dragging the unwilling Ray, who shuffled lest he fall. The gutted stomach connected to sagging, deflated breasts below a neck with a bony hand clamped around it. Ray gagged. The angel was a woman. *Once.* Her face had decomposed, the edges of her orifices blackened with putrefaction. Milky-white eyes oozed viscous gel and stared at them silently. The hand around her throat twitched, and the mouth muscles moved. Her voice was perfect.

"*I'm sorry, so sorry. I can't leave no matter how hard I try.*"

Their eyes followed the hand, connected to a spindly arm, elongated and stretching back to the wall cave, melding into black, rocky grottos.

"I just stepped through and then the door closed and now… Now I can't leave…"

The long arms towered high, the dead woman still talking. A puppet.

"It's worse when I'm hungry. I just can't think, my mind scatters. Time scatters." Slender shadows on the ceiling of many long arms reached from all corners of the cave connecting to a pot of ink sticking to the roof. The corpse's vocal cords began crying. *"I'm stuck in this cave, all outta time and too much of it."*

Transfixed, the pitch lowered, its shape nebulous and morphing, like it was at all ages of growth and none at all. A black cloud abruptly shrinking, or growing with spindly, numerous legs. It lowered, and Ray imagined the blue jewel eyes he had never seen. The monster spoke through the dead. *"It's better when I'm full though. Hunger is chaos. The hungry world, no matter what world, is always chaos."*

The black cloud congealed, lowering to their eyeline. A petrified Leon finally remembered his saber just as a finger and talon curled around his head, slicing his cheek open. Another three hands plucked him from the hill and down into the darkness. while one more emerged, reaching for Ray just as he was blinded by blue light and time spun him away.

Ray paused a step inside the entrance, sick with vertigo and disorientated. He had forgotten something. Leon stepped ahead, his bravado nearly faltering. The cave's decline was immediate, the innards were a chasm. Down and through, with no bottom they could see.

The woman spoke, *"I've been stuck down here for an age."*

Leon mumbled, navigating the hill, "What you doing down here…?"

She interrupted, her voice now positively exuberant. *"Oh God, I thought no one would find me. Everyone passes and no one stays. Nothing stays. Even time leaves."*

A breath on Ray's nape transfigured his feet to steel blocks, a looming awareness of a presence hiding in the dark. When he finally spoke, his voice was strange and held a duplexity to it. "Anyone else down here?"

Leon paused and looked at him curiously.

The woman didn't reply, as if studying Ray in the darkness, and the sensation of hands, eyes, grew, suddenly interested in Ray. A weight bloomed in his chest, making it heavy, his throat burning from icy-hot liquid he hadn't yet drank. A monster loomed above them, clinging to the ceiling, he was sure of it.

The woman gasped, *"Thief!"* just as Ray's headache flared with the incandescent light, causing him to convulse. Time pounded memories into his slow mind, playing catch-up. The corpse, the monster, blood oozing down his throat, curdling onto his being.

Unthinking, Ray immediately retreated one step into the sunlight, out of the cave's influence. Out from *its* unnatural, unworldly, chaotic asynchrony, the voice *thief* reverberating through the cave like time played it on repeat.

Leon's smooth brow furrowed at his partner, and he turned his back on the cave's darkness. Behind him, spindly white hands levitated out from the dark, connected to impossibly long white arms dipped in the black recesses. Fingers snatched Leon's head, a talon snaring his mouth like a fishhook, and sheared his cheek open. He screamed, the sound falling flat without a mouth. The antique saber clattered to the ground, forgotten. Other hands, white and alien, gripped his body like a blanket of fingers and lifted Leon like a child, submerging him into the cave's Stygian depths. Leon's shriek was suddenly cut off.

Blue light exploded like fireworks inside Ray's head and eyes and brain. He clutched his skull, curling onto the ground, listening to Leon shriek again. Off and on, howling, always severed only suddenly to return. Like Leon jumped through time. Being eaten in the wrong order. Until there was nothing. Silence.

The flaring light slowed in Ray's brain, the sounds, his panic, his heart, all calming. He blinked his eyes open. His bifocals had fallen and lay on the ground, right next to Leon's fancy saber. He picked both up as he stood and looked to the cave. A shadow moved in the darkness, watching Ray silently. Ray gripped the saber as if he knew how to use it, his heart starting another race, when a pale, naked body floated within the murk. It was Leon, naked, skin gray and weeks into decomposition, a black hole in his belly, and milky white eyes in his head. The carcass hung limp, suspended by the hand gripping his throat.

The hand and fingers twitched, and Leon's mouth opened for his silver tongue and charm. His voice crooned in echoes, flowed through time like a river of darkness. The gray corpse, levitating in the dark, sang.

That old-time religion...

It's good enough for me...

Ray ran, his new saber clutched at his side.

TO DIE A MONSTER

by Samuel Poots

I try to scream as it pulls me from its walls, but my vocal cords haven't formed yet. It stitches me together, thread by thread, muscle and skin and bone snapping into place, until at last I stumble to the floor. By the time my voice is ready, it's too late. The house has my mind.

A steady knocking reaches my ears. "Hello? Anyone home? I have glassware for sale. Herbs. Saints' bones and all manner of minerals."

The house brings me to my feet. I try to fight, but it bats aside my efforts. A newly formed bone, inexpertly made, cracks the second I put weight on it. The house makes me walk anyway, has me put on clothes then go to the door, stringy umbilical ropes stretching from my shoulders to the flesh beneath its stone.

A little man stands before the door, mustache bristling beneath a red face and a gray cap. He blinks at me, one hand raised to knock again. The house has no words, so all I can do is wait.

"Oh. Good morning, sir. Sorry for hollering there."

I blink once. Inside I'm screaming. *Go! Run! Bring fire, bring axes! Here be monsters!* The words build in my throat, push against my teeth.

"Well, sir, I'm a peddler by trade. A purveyor of fine wares. I saw the Guild of Alchemists seal above your door and thought, 'There's someone who might be in need of a thing or two.' Eh?"

He grins, as though I am his best friend. The house stares blankly through my eyes. I want so desperately to return that smile, just to prove I'm not the monster.

His smile wavers. He looks down and coughs. "Is there anyone else I could talk to, perhaps?"

At last, the house stirs, bullying my thoughts down a new path. "Yes, of course. Come inside."

It steps me aside and has me open the door, careful to keep the strings at my back hidden from the peddler's sight.

Smile returning, the little man shoulders his pack and steps inside, nodding and thanking me.

As I close the door behind him, he's hit with the smell of rotting corpses. Ever the salesman, he tries to think of something nice to say even as my hands close around his neck. I push him against the wall.

Stones in the wall open like teeth to reveal pulsing, festering flesh. The peddler tries to scream, to fight, but he is a little man and I was once a fisherman, used to hauling heavy nets all day. I think that's why the house uses me for this. I stare into his eyes, trying to let him know I'm sorry, this isn't my fault, I have no choice, but the gesture is wasted. There's nothing but fear in his eyes now, and pretty soon, I feel his soul join us as the house swallows him whole. His soul disappears into a dark sea, made from a hundred captive minds, and his body is stripped of its flesh. Skin and muscle flow away beneath the walls, while his bones become part of the foundation. And since the house no longer needs me, it drags my mind back into the sea with him.

This is how it always goes.

I don't know what the house is. I don't think any of us know. It looked old even when I first found it, back when I knocked on its door to sell fish to the motherly figure it used as bait. Not even the house seems to remember its age. Perhaps, somewhere beneath the many layers of people taken, there is someone, the first one, who knows what the house was before it took root. Sometimes, when the house focuses its hunger elsewhere, I catch glimpses of something. A world distorted behind glass. Hands cradling me, telling me something. Something about protection. But it soon gets consumed in the roaring sea of souls.

We howl without voices from beneath the floorboards, groan in pain from out the walls. The rafters are our rib cage, the stone our skin. The house pulses beneath and between it all, a great beating heart made from our stolen meat.

I fall to the ground like a landed fish. Stones chatter against one another as they furl back in behind me, leaving exposed only those fleshy strings connecting us. How long has it been since it last gave me form? Not long, surely. I can still feel the house feeding on the poor peddler, his mind growing ragged in my thoughts.

The cold air cuts like a knife. I can taste the memory of snow. Nighttime shadows pour down the empty hearth and pool in the house's corners. A single window looks out onto the street, but there's so much grime on the glass that even the moon is turned into a silver smudge. Everything is silent and still. Why has the house called me up?

The door settles against its hinges. Then someone sneezes.

I'm pulled to my feet, and I see a shadow through the gaps in the warped planks. Someone is sleeping on our steps. And the house, ever hungry, wants them.

It drags me over to the peddler's clothes, dresses me even as new muscles worm beneath my skin. It remakes my body each time, grows it from stolen flesh. But it needs my mind. It doesn't know how to speak without a mind to puppet.

As I struggle with the shirt buttons, I realize something is different this time. I'm not quite what I should be. My movements are clumsy, my thoughts more my own. The house is still there, still pulling the strings, but it feels…lazy, as though puppeteering me with only one hand. It takes me three tries to open the door.

And there he lies: a beggar, shivering beneath a scrap of cloak. Little more than sackcloth, really. I stare at him, admiring the way the moonlight picks out his dark curls, the curve of his lip. In another life, perhaps…

The wind cries. The man whimpers into his cloak.

So alone. So hungry and alone, a voice whispers.

I jump at the sound. My head whips around, but there's no one there. I look at the beggar, but he's still asleep. *I just moved my head.*

Take him, the voice whispers again.

It's the house. I've never heard it before. How can I? It uses our voices. But why now? What's happened?

I don't move. And it doesn't make me.

Take him!

Searching for answers, I do something I've never done before. I explore our connection. With my body to anchor me, it's like standing on the edge of a great abyss. I look down into it, upon minds wrapped in and around themselves, wailing and clawing at one another in our anguish. It all washes over me, tearing my mind's edges, threatening to pull me back into that sea. Somehow, I keep my ground and grit my teeth against the pull. That's what lies within the house's being.

There! Amidst the many minds, I spy the peddler. He's not a brave man. Not a strong man. But his presence is still fresh enough to draw the house's attention. It has wrapped itself around him, an amorphous thing of stolen voices and endless appetite. The part of it which reaches me now is just a fraction, a piece small enough for me to hear its individual voice.

The wind blows across my skin, calling me back. Dry leaves rattle down the street. The sleeping beggar mumbles and turns over, the moon shining full upon his youthful face.

He doesn't matter. This is my chance. I stare out at the empty street, feel my legs tense beneath me, ready to run. I will not die a monster.

The skin on my back bursts into flame. I hear the familiar sound of chattering stone as the flesh-ropes tighten to reel me back in. The house knows something is wrong. I resist. I attempt to pull my body free, biting down against the pain. Despite it, I'm nearly laughing. I'm commanding my body. Me! Somewhere inside that dark sea of souls, the peddler screams, and the house tears its attention away to focus on me.

Little time remains, but I can still do something.

I pull off the peddler's jacket. It is well-made and warm, perhaps the most precious thing he owned.

The skin on my back is pulled like pine tar. The flesh-strings haul me back, but not before I bundle up the jacket and throw it at the sleeping figure. My aim is good, and he shoots to his feet, as frightened as a startled rabbit. His eyes meet mine.

The house retakes control of me.

Calmly, it nods my head and closes the door. Then it turns me on my heel and walks me back across the floor. The wall opens up to welcome me back into its hellish embrace, but as my body is slowly broken down and my mind returns to the sea of captives, I smile.

I woke the beggar up. He got away. I'm not the monster.

The house wraps itself jealously about me, shoving me deep beneath its captured minds. Clawing, screaming, endless, maddened minds. And I scream with them. Our cries are the wind passing through the chimney, the creak of the floorboard, the chink and scrape of settling stone. The monster, which wears the building like a mask, moves with our fear and pain.

I wish I were dead. Dead and nothing. Oblivion is better—far better—than this. I try to fight my way free. My mind flinches as other thoughts pass through it. I drag them out of me, keep myself apart, tear at these other minds with imagined claws and teeth. I have tasted freedom. I cannot let it go. I will not!

But the minds pile in on mine and soon I am crushed beneath them, their selves mixing with mine, a thousand droplets running together to form a sea.

An image flickers past. A memory. I'm not sure if it's mine or someone else's. The docks. Fishing nets dragging through my fingers. A wooden bucket in which things scrabble. Crabs. *No lid is needed,* our father says. The crabs struggle to keep each other down, too caught up in themselves.

The memory fades. I drown in the sea.

I emerge again to hear a knocking sound, and the house's control wraps tight around me. A dozen captive minds cling to me like fog, but as soon as the house puts me in my body, their voices are snuffed out. There is only the house, and this time, it holds its connection, its need flowing into me through the strings.

The knocking comes again. A face appears at the grime-covered window. They smear the dirt with a sleeve and try to peer inside. I get an impression of long, black hair and pale features.

Oh no. No, no, no. He can't have come back. I saved him, I woke him up, the house didn't get him!

The face disappears, and the knocking resumes. The hunger rises in me, through me, as the house pushes me forward, forces me into clothes and to the door.

No. Not again. I won't be a monster again. I won't!

I lock my muscles up, but they are muscles made from the house. I am its body, just as it is mine. It pushes my shuffling steps forward. It's desperate. Even with everyone it has taken, it is still desperate.

The beggar stands before the door, outlined in the predawn gloom. He smiles like a man who has forgotten how. In his hands, he clutches the peddler's jacket.

"Hello. I'm…This is yours, yes?"

I clamp my jaw shut. The house creaks its frustration. It nods my head.

The man looks down at the jacket, then he thrusts it back out to me. "Thank you, sir. It was very welcome during the night, but…I don't want charity. I know your heart is in the right place, but I can't take this. You don't look much better off than I do." He casts his eyes around the house—at its cracked and crumbling walls, at its small windows and deep, dust-filled shadows. "Is this house yours? Or…"

The question hangs in the air. I try not to think, not to let my mind dwell on what the missing words could mean, but meaning comes regardless. He thinks I'm a squatter. Just another beggar like him, but with enough good luck to find this run-down alchemist's house sitting empty.

The house reads the thought and twists my lips up into a welcoming smile. "No. I found it empty." I open the door a little wider, the house still careful to keep its connection to me hidden behind. "You're welcome in, if you need shelter today."

The man takes half a step forward, then hesitates. He eyes me. This is someone who has survived this city's streets, where body snatchers stalk the alleys in search of body parts to sell the alchemists. Suspicion and paranoia are hard habits to break. I stare back, willing him to flee. Surely, he can tell something is wrong here.

The wind gusts past, sudden and sharp. He shivers. "Alright," he says. "But so you know, I've got a knife."

The house nods my head and steps me back to let him enter.

He steps across the threshold, and immediately the house rises up to meet him. Biting mouths and grasping hands push flagstones out of their way. They take hold of the man's foot. He doesn't even have time to scream before I am upon him, too, pushing him to the ground, where the house opens its floors to greet him.

A line of fire drags across my chest. Hot, black ichor spatters the floor and white-hot pain explodes inside my skull.

The beggar has his knife out. He slashes me again, then stabs the blade upward through my bicep. A feeling like ice water pours down my arm, leaving wretched, tingling numbness in its wake. The house feels it too. Rafters splinter, exposing bone and muscle inside the wood, but still, it does not let me release its prey.

The beggar is sinking into the floor now. Fleshy tentacles crawl over him, cover his mouth, his nose, his eyes. I sink down with him, feeling him begin to slip into our sea of souls.

He panics. His arm flails, knife blade flashing. Again, that burning lash of fire. Something tears free from my back, and the house is gone.

I fall hard to flagstones, which move like the deck of a ship at sea. All around me, faces push their way through the walls, half-made hands clawing at the air. The faces wail with pain. I can feel it, but its muted, distant.

The strings. I reach back and find them hanging from my shoulders, dripping more black ichor from severed ends. The beggar cut me free! I stumble to my feet, laughing. I can laugh again! I cry, I laugh, I scream, I make every noise I can because, by the gods, I'm free!

But then my leg buckles, and I fall to one knee. Numbness spreads up my uninjured arm, and I look down to find the skin sloughing away. I am a dead thing, a mind stuffed into a meat puppet. Without the house, I'm falling apart.

But I will not die a monster. I climb again to my feet. I see the door. The floor rocks, tries to trip me up, but I was a fisherman, I know how to walk through a storm.

I am nearly to the exit when something catches my foot. It's his leg. The man who cut me free. He's nearly gone beneath the writhing viscera, but still, he fights, weak legs kicking wildly.

The door beckons to me. An open street lies beyond. A place to die as myself. I will not die a monster.

Cursing, I reach down and grab the man's legs. To my amazement, he starts to come free. The house is all-consuming, but it is not strong. It needs us to be its strength.

Arms burst from the floor, pulling the beggar from my grip. I don't have enough strength in my rotting muscles to contend with all of them. All I can do is watch as the man is dragged back into the house's grasp.

A hand seizes my ankle. I look down into a skinless, blood-streaked face. A mind touches mine, filled with agony and fear. It is trying to claw its way out, but really, it is only dragging me back down with it. While trying to free myself, I remember the bucket filled with crabs. No prison is needed when they fight one another for freedom.

I grab the hand and let myself flow back down into that sea of souls.

Our minds are swarming. The house is piling us on top of its latest victim, filling us with hunger. Its attention is far from me right now.

I'm not sure what I'm doing, but I let my assailant's mind into mine. She's a sad, gibbering thing, someone who spent far longer in this darkness than me. I share with her my thoughts. I show her the way out.

In response, her hand claws up my leg, and I help it. A shoulder follows. Then a head, wrapping itself in raw flesh. She cannot make skin, hair, or teeth. Those abilities are beyond us. But soon, her body breaks free. She stumbles upright, eyes wide, crying bloody tears. Then, without a word to me, she turns and staggers out the door.

There's no time to wonder what will happen to her. I let myself fall back into the sea, so I can help the next one. And the next one. And the next one. More and more come, bodies clambering out, piecing themselves together, escaping as a shambling, screaming, joyful horde. Most flee, but some stay to help free ourselves from ourselves. And with each mind freed, the house is weakened.

Suddenly, I feel the house take hold. I fall, ribs splintering, skull cracking. It wraps itself around my mind, crushes me with the sheer weight of its attention. It tries to shove my awareness down below the minds it has taken, but there are now fewer to drown me in. My awareness swims through the darkness until I stand again in that abstract ocean of thought and misery. Minds surround me, and I brace myself for the worst, but they do not fight me. Instead, they carry me to the ones still pulling us free. For a second, I'm back in my body, watching as the beggar drags himself out and flees with the others. Then the thing which lives within the house cries and pulls me to its center.

The darkness is empty. There are no other souls left. I hang suspended there, listening to silence. Endless emptiness envelops me. I have forgotten how beautiful it is to be alone.

Not entirely alone. I hear weeping, like a baby. I stretch out to it, and for a moment, I see through the eyes of my jailer, trapped in a glass jar, the only home it had, cradled by a man, its creator. He named it Homunculus. Gave it a duty: to protect all that was his. Then he poured out his tiny creation and, with its flesh, mortared his home. After he died, his soulless creation was alone.

The half-formed mind looks up at me.

Stay. Stay. So alone.

"Do you want to leave?" I ask at last.

The little mind settles in next to mine and lets itself dissolve into my thoughts. It never had a body, not a real one, so I share mine.

When I open my eyes, there is only us inside the house. Stone walls, their flesh mortar gone, are breaking apart.

I stumble over to the door so the homunculus can look through my eyes to the world outside. It's a bright, crisp morning. The street is filled with skinless corpses. Some have already fallen apart, others are dying, with their flayed heads turned toward the sun. We are free. All of us.

I collapse as I cross the threshold, and the house collapses with me.

He finds me later, the man who slept outside our door. My savior. My flesh has almost completely unraveled, my lower half buried beneath stones and timber.

He looks down at me. There's not enough life left in me to close my eyes. That face, that beautiful, gaunt face, hunger-pinched and frostbitten, twists with disgust, fear, and hate. And fascination. He bends down, tries to get a better look at me without coming too close. He looks at me the way someone looks at a monster.

The thought almost makes me smile. I can't blame him. It will be my face in his nightmares. Not a crumbling prison for a sad, lonely creature. I curl my thoughts around what's left of the homunculus.

The beggar shudders, then produces a tinder box.

A scrape. A spark. Then fire.

Before long, my skin is peeling away like paper, and my eyes are crumbling into dust.

I sigh and sink into my true death. I'm happy to be his monster.

AUTHOR INTERVIEW

PAUL TREMBLAY

Feature by Janelle Janson

Recently I had a chance to chat with renowned horror author Paul Tremblay. Not only does he write thoughtful characters the reader can invest in, his ambiguously styled storytelling will keep you thinking long after you finish. In this insightful exchange, we delve into Paul's creative process, his venture into film with *Knock at the Cabin*, and his tantalizing upcoming projects. It's an intriguing journey, offering a peek into the life and inspirations of an author who persistently redefines the contours of the horror genre.

JANELLE JANSON: Paul, thank you again for taking the time to chat with me. I am a superfan and have to pinch myself whenever I get the opportunity to do this. Briefly, can you introduce yourself?

PAUL TREMBLAY: Thank you, Janelle. Well, I'm Paul. I like reading books and watching sports in my spare time. I've been a high school math teacher for *years redacted*. I've also written a bunch of books, including *A Head Full of Ghosts*, *The Cabin at the End of the World*, and *The Pallbearers Club*. Despite what John Langan claims, I do not plan on murdering him.

JJ: That's good to know. Do you have any superstitions or rituals when you write? Where do you find inspiration?

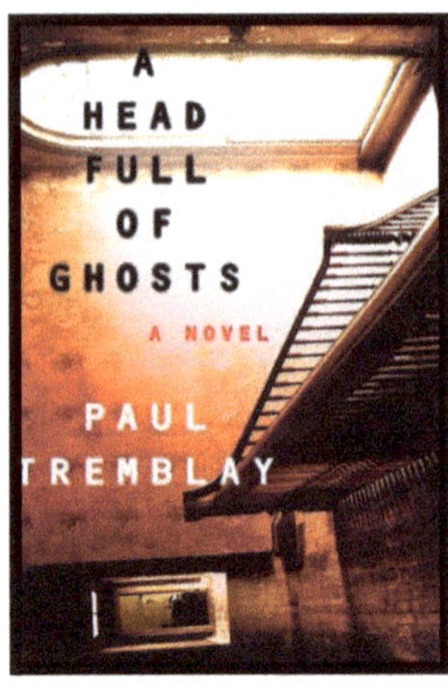

PT: No superstitions (knock on wood) or rituals. I don't have time for rituals, especially during the school year. If I find a free hour, then I sit my butt down and take advantage of it.

As far as inspiration goes… *Everything?* The most common sources of inspiration come from books, music, movies. When a book/song/movie lands with me, I get excited, and I think, *oh, I want to try that,* or *I want to get close to that in some way, using a spark to build a new fire.* Of course, inspiration can be totally random—an as-you-go-about-your-day thing. I try to remain open to those moments when something minor happens and it bubbles into a what-if-scenario. So yeah, fire and bubbles.

JJ: What are you currently reading and loving? Any books coming out that you're excited about?

PT: I'm about to dive into a few non-fiction books for novel research (ugh, I hate research). But I'm currently reading Stephen King's *Holly,* which is excellent. I'm looking forward to reading Rachel Harrison's *Black Sheep,* Chuck Wendig's *Black River Orchid,* and Tananarive Due's *The Reformatory.* I had the opportunity to read an early copy of *A Haunting on the Hill* by Elizabeth Hand, a novel set in Shirley Jackson's *Hill House.* That book will be published later in October, and I'm sure folks will love it as much as I did.

JJ: I have to say, you have amazing taste in books. Please tell us a bit about your latest book, *The Beast You Are.* Was this a collection of stories you recently wrote? Or were these stories written over several years?

PT: The title of the collection references the loose theme of monsters and monstrousness. Not every one of the fifteen stories has a literal monster in them, but many do. In the other stories, the characters confront the monsters of grief or their own monstrous actions and selves. While there is the loose theme connecting the stories, I hope that each story is its own monster and doing its own thing.

The bulk of the stories were first published after my 2019 collection *Growing Things and Other Stories,* but a few stories are older, with "The Blog at the End of the World" (first published in 2009) as the oldest. The title novella is brand spanking new.

JJ: Which story stands out most to you? For the record, I loved every single one. "The Postal Zone," "The Dead Thing," "House of Windows," "The Last Conversation," and the title story really stuck with me. It's almost impossible to pick a favorite.

PT: Thank you for the kind words. Each story claims a plot of land in my heart, but the novella, "The Beast You Are," is my favorite, or the one that has the largest plot of land. I had a blast writing it, and there's a part of me that can't believe I wrote it—in a good way! Getting to engage or converse with some of my favorite works (*Watership Down, Secrets of NIMH,* Toby Barlow's *Sharp Teeth,* Chris Ivrin's *Ragged*) was a true pleasure. "The Beast You Are" was a rare story idea that I let hang around and marinate for a few years before attempting to write it, mainly because I didn't think my publisher would consider publishing an anthropomorphic animal novel written in free verse. But when they asked me for a collection, I thought I could sneak it into the world as a novella.

So many of the images and characters from "The Beast You Are" remain vividly fresh in my head. Magg and Mereth will be hanging out with me for a long time, I think.

JJ: *The Rats of NIMH* and *Watership Down* are two of my favorites. Do you enjoy writing short fiction, long fiction, or both? Do you schedule your writing time?

PT: I like both. When I first started writing, I wrote nothing but short stories. But now that I've been in novel mode for about ten years, I find it more challenging to return to shorts. When I do return to short stories, the experience is (generally) enjoyable (or as enjoyable as writing is for me), informative, and even restorative. It's nice to take a 2-4 week break from the novel in progress to work on a short piece. Then, when I get back to the novel, I usually come back with

fresh eyes. We all want fresh eyes, right? And we all want fire and bubbles too, apparently.

During the school year, my writing time, it's a day-to-day kind of thing, where I try to find an hour or two for writing, or writing-related activities. Sometimes I can steal a period for writing at school, though usually, I'm working at night. On off-days, I prefer to work in the morning.

JJ: I'm so curious: how was the entire experience making *Knock at the Cabin*? Can you share any insights into the process of collaborating with M. Night Shyamalan and the translation of your story to the big screen?

PT: The experience was exciting, dizzying, but also frustrating at times with the weird (to carefully choose a word) lack of support or acknowledgment of the book prior to the film's release. Not to mention the amount of hassle they gave us over the media-tie-in edition of the book, so, I um, won't mention it.

JJ: Yes, I was one of those annoying book people shouting on my social media. But I won't mention that either.

PT: As far as insights into the collaboration goes, there are none, because it wasn't a collaboration. Which was and is fine. I knew going in that I wouldn't be consulted or anything like that on screenplay or story decisions. Visiting the set for two days and going with my family to the premiere were certainly exciting and wonderful experiences that will stay in the memory palace until it collapses into rubble.

JJ: Are there any other works of yours that you'd like to see adapted into film, and if so, which stories?

PT: I'd love to see many more adaptations of my work, of course. *Survivor Song* is currently the closest to being a flickering image thing.

JJ: Is there any chance *A Head Full of Ghosts* will be adapted to screen? I know there has been some talk.

PT: Yeah, there's a chance. It's under option currently, but there aren't as many pieces in place as there are for *Survivor Song*. We'll see. Fingers crossed.

JJ: While we're on the topic, what book by another author would you like to see adapted into a film or television series?

PT: I'd love to see John Langan's *The Fisherman*, Mariana Enriquez's *Our Share of Night*, and Sarah Langan's *Good Neighbors* as limited series. I think we're getting an adaptation of Liz Hand's *Generation Loss*, so that's very exciting. Give me Gabino Iglesias's *The Devil Takes You Home* as a movie. Also, I'd love to see a limited series of Bolano's *The Savage Detectives* and/or *2666*. Oh, and I volunteer to write the screenplay adaptations of Cynan Jones's *The Dig* and Peter Straub's "Mr. Clubb and Mr. Cuff."

JJ: What is a book you like to reread? What book really scares you?

PT: I wish I had more time (don't we all) for rereads. For about a ten-year period, I used to reread Kurt Vonnegut's *Slaughterhouse Five* each June. That's the book I've reread the most. I like to squeeze in some King rereads by audiobook. This year, I've reread *The Fisherman* and *Our Share of Night*.

I don't know if I can pick one or think of one singular book that scares me the most. Beyond the scary works I've already mentioned, let's add Sara Gran's *Come Closer* to the list.

JJ: Do you have anything else you'd like to tell us about? Any new projects in the works?

PT: My novelette "In Bloom" was recently published by Amazon Original Stories as a part of the *Creature Feature* collection. I'm about to turn in copy edits for my novel *Horror Movie*, which will publish June 25, 2024. And I wrote a middle grade novel that I hope to have some news on soon.

My newest project is a calculus quiz, and I just realized that I gave them some problems that weren't supposed to be on the quiz. Every math student's nightmare, yeah?

The Beast You Are is currently available for purchase wherever books are sold.

REPRINT STORY

Originally Published as "Close Your Eyes" in Mythic Magazine

ONE LAST STEP

by Warren Benedetto

"**W**ill it hurt?" I watched my father roll the sewing needle between his fingers, the tip glowing orange-red in the heat of the flame. My eyes welled with tears.

"Just a little," he replied.

The flickering candlelight sent eerie shapes dancing around the cluttered attic, where we were hiding for the night. Outside, the screeching calls of the shadow-things rose and fell like whale songs made from rusted metal. They sounded close.

My father removed the needle from the fire, blew on it, then pinched it quickly a few times between his fingertips to check the temperature. Satisfied that it wasn't too hot, he dipped the tip into the puddle of royal-blue ink he had spilled from a broken ballpoint pen. "All right. Give me your arm."

"Can I hold Roger?" I pointed to the stuffed rabbit leaning against a dusty cardboard box.

"Of course." My father bent down and picked up the toy. He handed it to me. "Squeeze him tight, okay? This might take a minute."

I nodded, then tentatively extended my arm. My father turned my wrist toward the ceiling so that my forearm was facing up. After dipping the needle in the ink again, he poked the sharp tip into my skin. I winced, then jerked my arm away.

"Ow! It hurts!"

"I know. I'm sorry. But we have to do this, just in case."

"In case of what?"

My father's eyes glimmered in the candlelight. He pressed his lips together in a sad smile. "It's just important you remember, okay?" His voice was scratchy. His throat sounded tight. I nodded. "Can we try again?"

He grasped my wrist and stretched my arm out straight. A whimper escaped my lips as he brought the needle close to my skin.

"Hey," he said gently. He looked me in the eyes. "What do we do when we're scared?"

"We go inside."

"That's right. Can you do that now?"

"Okay." I searched my mind for a happier time, before the shadow-things. I focused on the details—the sounds, the smells, the colors—until the memory was as vivid as the day it first happened.

"Good." My father dipped the needle into the ink once again. "Now, close your eyes."

My lemon-yellow rain boots splashed into a giant puddle on the side of the road. A steady drizzle fell from the smudged charcoal sky, plastering my hair to the side of my face and soaking the dirty stuffed rabbit I clutched in one tiny hand.

I navigated around the husk of an abandoned car overturned on the shoulder of the road, momentarily straying over the white line and into the lane. It didn't matter, no cars were coming. Not anymore. I could barely remember the last time I had seen one driving.

As I passed the wreckage, I ran my fingers along the telltale gashes sliced through the side of the car. The damage ran the length of the vehicle, from the front wheel to the taillight. Something had cut through the metal like it was made from soft clay. I examined the edge of the gashes. They were rusty. That was good—it meant the damage had happened a while ago. The shadow-thing that had attacked the car was probably long gone.

I dropped to my hands and knees to peek through the shattered driver's-side window, hoping to find something useful inside: food, maybe, or a cigarette lighter. A blanket. A gun. But there was nothing, just a rosary in heap upon the upside-down roof, beads still coiled around the cracked rearview mirror.

I sat back on my heels and wiped the water out of my eyes. I was soaked. I wished my raincoat still had a hood, but my father had cut it off ages ago.

It was too dangerous, he said. It blocked my peripheral vision. I would need to see, in case the shadow-things attacked from the side. They usually did.

Usually.

At the thought of my father, I slid up the sleeve of my raincoat to reveal part of the tattoo he had hand-lettered on my forearm. I mouthed the words as I read them.

1. *Run.*

2. *Hide.*

3. *Close your eyes.*

"This is your mantra," my father had explained, as he pressed the ink-tipped needle into my skin. "This is how you survive. Just remember to do these things, and I promise you'll be safe."

I hadn't understood at the time. Why did I need it tattooed on my arm? Why couldn't he just tell me to run when I needed to run, like he always did when the shadow-things came? The two of us would hide together, our eyes squeezed shut to avoid the monsters' deadly gaze, waiting until the creatures gave up searching for us and moved on to easier prey.

A few months later, I found out why.

My father and I had done everything perfectly: we ran, we hid, we closed our eyes. But that day, for whatever reason, my father had opened his eyes just a little too soon. It was only for a split second—barely more than a blink—but it was enough time for the shadow-thing to burrow into his mind, to draw him out, to steer him helplessly into the open like some sort of puppet.

I didn't see what happened, but I felt it: the rush of air as the shadow-thing swung its blade, the wet squelch of the scythe eviscerating my father's body, the warm spray of his blood slapping across my face. Through it all, I kept my eyes closed. When I finally opened them, my father was nowhere to be found. All that remained was a dark stain on the ground, with drag marks that trailed into the woods and disappeared into the undergrowth. He was gone. And I was alone.

I felt a sob building in my chest. I didn't want to be alone; I wanted to be home. I wanted to be in my backyard, swinging on the swings while my father cooked dinner on the grill. He'd be wearing his apron—the one that said "World's Okayest Dad"—flipping burgers with one hand while taking swigs from a can of Diet Coke with the other. I'd hear my brother sloshing in the baby pool while my mother nursed my newborn sister on the lawn chair nearby. We'd be together again, as a family. All of us. Alive.

A gust of wind drove a blast of stinging raindrops against my face. The rain was falling harder. Before long, it would be a full-blown monsoon. I looked through the broken car window again. Water had pooled in the angled corner of the crushed windshield, but the back half of the car was dry. It would be a good shelter from the storm.

I crawled inside, clutched my stuffed rabbit to my chest, and listened to the thunder as it rolled through the hills.

It was still light outside when I awoke. I had dozed off, but not for very long by the looks of it. The downpour had subsided to a light gray sprinkle. A low ground fog drifted along the asphalt outside.

My stomach rumbled. I had to keep moving, to find another abandoned house or store from which I could scavenge some food. I would hunt if I had to—I had done it before—but I was hoping to find a cache of canned goods instead. My father had warned me that hunting should always be my last resort. It was dangerous. I could be hurt, even killed.

With my stuffed rabbit in hand, I crawled out through the car window and into the road. I looked to my left and my right, checking for anything dangerous that might be approaching me from the sides. There was nothing. Satisfied that I was in the clear, I stood, yawned, and stretched my arms towards the sky.

Suddenly, my yawn was cut short by an unexpected sound.

A splash.

Behind me.

I froze, listening.

The patter of raindrops on my jacket sounded like a thousand tiny footsteps approaching from all directions. But under that, there was something else. A scraping sound. Heavy and metallic, the sound of a blade dragging along the ground.

The shadow-thing.

I heard my father's voice in my head.

Run.

I didn't hesitate. I bolted down the road, sprinting straight ahead at first, then curving into the parking lot of a gas station on my right. My rain boots slapped on the ground, sending great geysers of muddy water up to my knees as I leaped over the median and slipped between the gas pumps. Something crashed behind me. An alien shriek of pain and rage pierced my eardrums. The sharp smell of gasoline stung my nostrils. I didn't look back.

The bottom half of the gas station door was shattered. I ducked through the opening, my boots crunching on broken glass as I entered. It took a moment for my eyes to adjust to the dim light of the convenience store. The shelves were empty. The doors of the coolers stood open. A pair of bare feet, their skin mottled and gray, protruded from the end of one of the aisles. A dark red chunk of one heel was missing, seemingly gnawed by some type of rodent.

Hide.

I scrambled behind the cashier's counter. The doors of the cabinet under the cash register were open. I pulled myself into the cramped space, then drew the doors closed behind me.

The cabinet was dark except for a sliver of light that slipped through the crack between the doors. I clutched my stuffed rabbit to my chest, then buried my face in its filthy fur and tried to muffle the ragged rasp of my breathing.

My heart pounded in my ears. I listened for the sound of the shadow-thing.

Broken glass crunched. The metallic scraping drew closer. The sharp odor of gasoline wafted through the air. A figure paused by the doors, blocking out the sliver of light. My ears reverberated with the guttural, resonant clicking of the shadow-thing. I recognized the sound. My father had called it "echolocation." It was searching for me.

Close your eyes.

I squeezed my eyes shut and willed myself to disappear, to fade into memory. To go inside, as my father used to say, losing myself in the happiest memory I could think of. The shadow-things couldn't touch me there. I would be safe.

I thought about the backyard: the smell of the grill, the splash of the pool, my brother's laugh, the wind in my hair as I swung on my swing, higher and higher, the whole world disappearing beneath me as I arced towards the brilliant blue sky...

The scraping started again. This time, it was moving away. The gasoline smell faded. After a while, all that was left was the gentle drumming of the rain on the roof overhead.

I opened my eyes and pressed my face to the thin seam of light between the cabinet doors. The shadow-thing was gone. Quietly, I slipped from the cabinet and crawled over to the gas station window. I could see the shadow-thing outside, its back turned to me, moving slowly towards the street.

My stomach rumbled again, cramping with hunger. I slid up the sleeve of my raincoat, again reading the tattoo my father had placed there.

1.   *Run.*

2.   *Hide.*

3.   *Close your eyes.*

I slid the sleeve further up my arm. There was one last step. It was written in a different ink, in a different color blue. It read:

4.   *Attack.*

My father had added it a few months after the first tattoo, shortly before he died. I remembered looking into his eyes as he pressed the needle into my skin.

"We aren't scared of them anymore?" I asked.

"We are. But now we know we can beat them. They're strong. But you're stronger. When the time is right, you know what to do."

I reached into my raincoat and drew out the long, curved blade that my father had salvaged from one of the shadow-things we had killed. Strips of purple rubber—the remnants from my raincoat hood—were wrapped around the handle. The blade was stained yellow-brown with the shadow-things' blood. It looked like mustard, but the taste was surprisingly sweet.

Especially when it was fresh.

My stomach growled again. I gripped the blade's handle in my fist, then propped my stuffed rabbit up into a sitting position in the window. I would need both hands free for what I had to do next.

"You wait here," I whispered to the rabbit. "When I get back, we'll make a fire." My eyes narrowed as I looked out the window at the shadow-thing. "Then, we'll eat."

FrostBite

Angela Sylvaine

AUTHOR AND ARTIST BIOS

For more information about the authors and artists featured in this issue, including bios, photographs, and web links to relevant work, please visit:

darkmattermagazine.shop/collections/halloween-special-issue-2023

SUBMIT TO DARK MATTER MAGAZINE

For more information on how to submit fiction or artwork to *Dark Matter Magazine*, please visit our submission guidelines page:

darkmattersubmissions.com

FRIENDS?

 Get our emails   

 Follow us on Twitter   

 Like us on Facebook   

 Follow us on Instagram